***Payback's A Bitch***

ISBN:0-9753966-0-9


Published by: 4Word Press
P.O Box 6411
Bridgeport, Connecticut 06606
www.4wordpress.com

Written by Marcus Spears for 4WordPress
Second 4 Word Press printing 2004
Printed in the United States of America.





For information regarding special discounts for bulk purchases and distribution please contact: (203) 373-1623 or
4 Word Press P.O Box 6411
Bridgeport, Connecticut 06606
or
WWW.4wordpress.com

Dedicated to
The cherished memory of
Auntie Pam

In addition to
my shinning Sun and the rest of
the fam in physical form as well
as in spiritual essence.

ONE LOVE

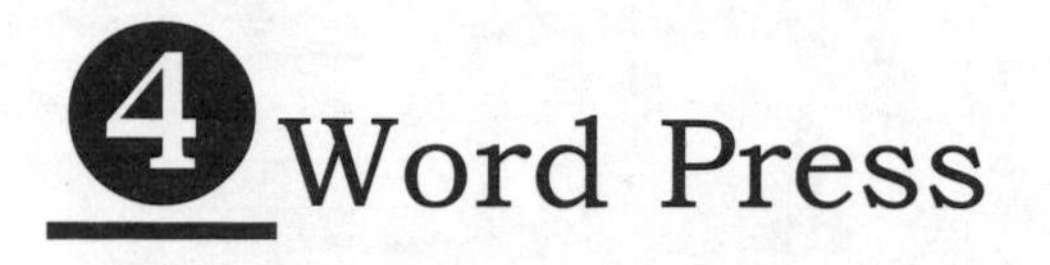


PRESENTS

# Payback's A Bitch

the first episode

A Novel by *Marcus Spears*

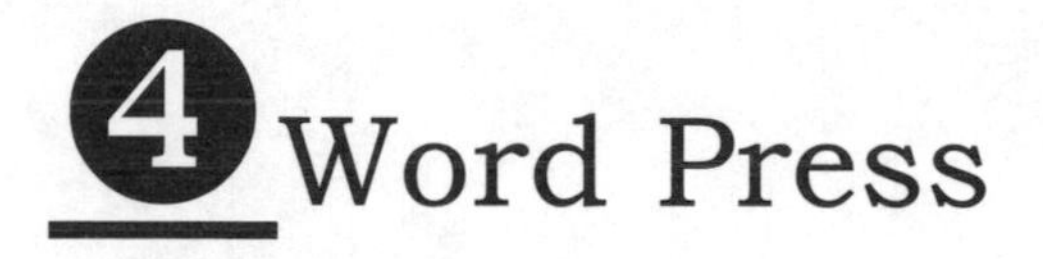


P R E S E N T S

# Payback's A Bitch

A Novel by *Marcus Spears*

## Shout outs

First and foremost I would like to give praise to the Great Cosmic Mother. Next I would like to give a tight hug and kiss to my favorite lady Donna Spears, peace ma I love you. Of course my other favorite woman, Coletta gets a tight hug and a wet kiss too, I love you cocolo lets get back to the crown chakra...together. To my Sun Amun who shines like one, daddy's in the building, easy on the smoothies! To my dearest Auntie Pam, Dutch misses you forreal, it just ain't the same. Get better uncle Les we got some fishin to do. To the rest of my Fam, *lean back* I got you.

Let me pour out my drink *east,* west, north and south to Kali, Ma'at, Lakini, Ra, Hathor, Sut, Heru, Brigit, Rudra, Agni, Nut, Shu, Shakti, Tara, Kakini, Oya, Xochiquetzal, Tehuti, Geb, Shiva, Amen Ra, Olo'dumare', Yemoja, Isis, Ausar, Palo, Sekmet, Sophia, Anpu, Min, El Cristo Negro and all others who dwell on the inside, Ashe'.

Lick a shot for all my PNC's on or not on the back of the Bridgeport Rest In Peace Basketball Tournament t-shirts, click, click, BOWW!

To all my fellow street vendors...we made this book game shit what it is WHΛT! Who was hustlin novels in 99? What'day know bout foldin tables and poppin trunks? Holla at ya boy.

To all the Black bookstores and distributors, *nuff respect.*

To authors like Teri Woods, Al' Saadiq Banks, Shannon Holmes and Steve Perry, to name a few, good lookin out on the book signings, whats really good? Holla.

Peace to the 4 Word Press staff...are those 90 days up yet, I'm gettin da shakes now, where we goin fo brekfis?

To all the authors out there who don't know that compared to music bizz we still in the Rakim/Kane stages of the book industry, this book shit's another phase of hip hop *do the knowledge when ya sign dem deals boy!*

Last but not least, one love to all the heads that copped this book. To the ones who even borrowed it from their friends...I ain't mad at you cause you read it at least, Peace.

**Marcus Spears**

# Introduction

**Bridgeport, Connecticut** the largest city in the state, a place where guns and bras are made in addition to record breaking murder rates; though to argue whose hood stacked the most bodies is nothing to brag about. The famous and one time Mayor of the city, *P.T Barnum,* was noted for stating that "There's a sucker born every minute." And sometimes your so called friends think you're one of those suckers. In these streets it's better to have enemies than it is to have friends...

# Scene One

*"Cloud Nine, two for tens! Two for tens" a 13 year-old kid hollered as he peeked his head around the side of building 11.*

*Like children with a sweet tooth eager to catch the ice cream man, crack heads ran from building to building once they heard Cloud Nine announced. It wasn't the most potent brand of base sold in the area, but it had to do since it was the only thing pumpin' after the heads across the street ran out. While matchstick looking fiends huddled around the naive boy running sales for the first time, his brand new Sony PlayStation Portable was being pick pocketed without notice.*

*"Nick-kay!" a girl called out, as she stood in front of the adjacent building watching every transaction.*

*"Yo Nikki!" the boisterous chick yelled again at the top of her lungs.*

*Tania stood at the door in slippers holding one of her children from the side hip impatient to enter the building.*

*"The damn buzzer's broke again," she hollered up to her friend, "can you come downstairs and let me in?"*

*Nikki leaned out of the bedroom window with an ear to the phone receiver. She had an extra long phone cord wrapped around her arm cursing someone out on the other end.*

*"Hold up Tania, I'll be down in a minute, Ronnie's on the phone...again!" Nikki shouted back, aggravated with her boyfriend calling from prison for the third time in one day.*

*Tania was upset as well, cause her children's father Drench, claimed that he didn't have any money for their son, but yet and still he was sitting in the parking lot rolling weed.*

*Just as Tania finished scribbling her new boyfriend's name on the plexi-glass window, some fat lady forcefully pushed the thick steel door open a moment after Tania moved her child out of harm's way. The fat lady with much attitude, barged out the door ignoring the young mama's threats to kick her ass, as she stormed toward the sidewalk to snatch her own six year-old from the curb like a rag doll.*

*"Get your narrow ass over here!" She rebuked, "Didn't I tell you to get me a pack of cigarettes before you start playing in the damn street...you little hard head muthafucka'!"*

*The fat lady was pissed off to no end as if her son should have considered her two pack a day smoking habit his main concern, rather than frolic in his already decaying childhood. The little boy screamed the entire time that his mother beat and yanked his ass back inside the brick complex.*

*Off to the side of building 10, were some children jumping up and down on an old pissy mattress. Their birdcall whistle alerted the older cats that were gathered around cars making drug sales that the police were on their way down the block.*

It was getting late in the day with activity increasing each second. Bananas wasn't even the word. There were like a million things happening at once inside the bowels of the Terrace Garden, one of the many constipated housing projects that populated Bridgeport.

As for the brother sitting in his truck watching everything go on, the background noise faded into concentration. Cream sat patiently in his brand new Yukon Denali for an hour already waiting for the small crowd assembled in front of building 9 to disperse. In the backdrop, a glowing orange sun seemed to be waving goodbye as Cream continued to scope everything through the crosshair of his eyesight.

Behind the declining ball of fire however, was dusk rolling in like a midnight marauder flexing tight leather gloves ready to ransack the projects. The parking lots and the curbsides in the Terrace Garden, "Garden" for short, were crowded with the usual suspects. Most of whom were either smoked out, looking for something to smoke or focused on making more money off of smoke.

Various females stood around adding themselves to the scenery, from thick pretty dimes parading their lustful bodies, to manly looking dyke chicks that didn't know which way they wanted to go. Many name-known gold diggers moved about sizing up the fancy $50,000+ vehicles that pulled in and out of the lots. To a passerby they would have thought public housing had valet parking from all of the people hopping in and out of the luxurious rides. Contrary to assumption the chatterbox crowds only appeared like they were having fun hanging out and bullshitting, but most heads were conducting business.

Cream stayed sunk in his black leather seat trying to remain unnoticed. Shaking his head side to side in reproach, Cream turned to the person sitting in the passenger side.

"I told you to empty that shit outside," he stated irritably, "I swear you're the sloppiest nigga in the world! And don't give me that I live here bullshit either. It already looks fucked up, take a look!"

Cream went on to let his boy Drench have it after he spilled tobacco all over the place, while gutting another one of his Garcia Vega cigars.

"Just watch what the fuck your doin' ai'ight? I just had this shit detailed," Cream affirmed.

Drench sat unnerved staring at the blunt he couldn't wait to puff as soon as the saliva dried off of it. Drench and Cream were somewhat close friends, but not as tight as they were when they attended high school together. It seemed now like D only hung around Cream when it was time to get paid.

Drench was a broke weed head that used to work at McDonalds, but got fired and arrested after he was caught selling ounces out of the drive-thru window. All he wanted to do was smoke and drink liquor nowadays, but when push came to shove Cream still had his back regardless of his stupidity.

"Not for nothing D, what good are you high before we even run up in the building? And don't spark that Vega until everything is over and done wit'."

Paused for a moment, they both watched an unmarked patrol car make a routine pass. Drench ignored the police as well as what Cream had just told him not to do and lit the blunt anyway.

"Fuck them punk ass rookies man, I paid for this smoke...maybe it looks fucked up out here cause you constantly throw shit out the window" said Drench, insinuating that his friend was responsible for all the trash that blew around after Cream spit his gum out the window.

Drench took a small toke of the weed snapping again like he really had a reason to be upset. He sounded silly, because he was the main one who always left a pile of cigar contents and empty cognac bottles wherever he went. Cream looked at him like he was slow in the head, completely fed up with his stupid remarks. They had business to tend to and this was not the time nor place to be playing games. The camel's back gave in, after Cream unintentionally inhaled a deep breath of the funny smelling weed smoke. To Drench's surprise he snatched the blunt from his lips with the reflex of a ninja as it took a few seconds for D's brain to register.

"This ain't a fuckin' game" Cream ranted, "I need all your mechanical skills intact! If you ain't on point now, how in the hell you gonna' watch my back when Tootsie's boyfriend shows up!"

Drench had a confused look on his face like Cream asked him to define The Unified Field Theorem. Cream was getting mad cause basically he was doing Drench a favor since Tania threatened to call Child Support on him. Drench stuck his head out the window like everything was everything, looking up at the project skyscraper in amazement as if he'd never seen the building before.

"Yo what the fuck is wrong with you today," Cream seriously questioned, before forcing his head back inside the truck.

Drench started rambling a mile a minute, smiling oddly as he deliriously went on and on.

"You should move out here Cream...*how tall you think that building is*? I feel like I could float to the top" he giggled, then started counting on his fingers all the different things for Cream to consider.

"We got money, hoes, guns, Dro, all types of gear from the boosters and yo," Drench conversed with himself, "don't forget about the drinks from Sandra's mother the bootlegger...we even got a Chinese restaurant next to a soul food spot nigga what! My hood is crunked out!" He yelled.

Cream wasn't stunned by his boy's psychotic behavior after he realized what was up. Drench was known for lacing his weed with angel dust and in Bridgeport, dust was commonly called "wet" or "leak" and since he smoked so much of it, he acquired the nickname "Drench" as in soaking wet or saturated with angel dust.

Cream thought for a second then abruptly started the ignition. While pulling out of the parking lot he contemplated whether or not to drop D off. This wasn't the first time Drench had a dust spasm and usually Cream just felt sorry for him knowing it was the drugs that made him act retarded, but in order to handle business feeling sorry wouldn't cut it this time.

At first Cream thought about replacing Drench. There was this loud mouth white boy he met in a card game named Geek that lived in the Garden, but he really didn't know the kid that well. Halfway out of the lot Cream remembered that Geek sold drugs time to time for some clown named Fat Jack. Jack was the main course on the menu so that idea was definitely out.

According to Cream's main man Warren Hawkins, Jack was an old trifling nigga who had a girlfriend living on the seventh floor in building 9 that needed to get got. Warren was the one who convinced Cream to help him invade the apartment, but now that Drench was bugging out, they simply needed a look out to stick to the original plan if at all possible. Going into the building alone would be risky, especially if the hallways were crowded with wanna' be thugs trying to get a rep for themselves. Then again having a dusted fool wielding a gun behind him was just as dangerous, Cream figured.

"Fuck it!" He said, thinking out loud as he did a one handed U-turn back into the parking lot.

He decided to just leave Drench in the truck as a look out, instead of using him as rearview hallway vision.

Drench was completely out of it now, talking fast and acting out over dumb shit. Cream placed his hand on his shoulder like a little league coach would do to an adolescent pitcher during a bad game.

"Listen up son, your gonna' have to sit this one out. The deal we had earlier is off cause you're too high right now to watch my back. *Shit* you can't even watch your own back smoking that leak. I want everything to go nice and smooth so you're gonna' have to stay here. You did it to ya'self. The good news is you could still make some money if you follow instructions."

Drench gave a disappointed look while taking a sip from his bottle trying to appear sobered up. Tania, his baby's mother, demanded that he hit her off with some money this week or she was notifying the state on his ass, so he listened.

"See, that's why you stay broke! You always wanna' get high before it's time," Cream shouted after Drench took a big gulp of brown juice.

In the middle of chastising his boy, Cream

lowered his voice when people started looking. Then his cell phone rang once and stopped. It was the signal for him to get upstairs and hit the apartment. Grabbing the .40 caliber that laid under his seat, Cream clicked off the safety, stuffing the pistol into his waistband. He then ruffled a shopping bag, while standing outside of his truck struggling with the sneaker box that was wedged between the front and back seats.

"If you spot Fat Jack or any of his crew," Cream said, "all I need you to do is play one of my CD's *loud*. Matter of fact here," he handed Drench the DJ Kay Slay mix CD.

"Remember, full blast. But only if you peep them niggas heading back to the building you got it?" Drench nodded like he understood.

Cream's Yukon had a sound system in it that could be heard blocks away, so if Drench played it loud enough it would alert him that trouble was on it's way upstairs. He flicked the potent dust blunt away as if it were a cigarette butt, watching it land in the fresh piss puddle streaming under his tire.

"Just don't zone out on me this time D. You do wanna' get paid don't you?" Cream voiced in a stern tone at the same time zipping up his jeans, "For real yo, don't forget what I said."

Drench took another sip from his half-pint Hennessy bottle wiping his mouth with his sleeve.

"I got you man" he garbled, "you know I'm on point when I'm nice off the Henrock baby!"

Cream gave him the 'yeah right' smirk, as he pulled down on his Negro league fitted cap concealing his identity a little more.

# Scene Two

**The lobby was finally empty**. Cream quickly entered building 9 hitting the staircase and jetting up to the seventh floor. There was no choice about taking the stairs because in most public housing projects the elevators seemed to only work sporadically, sort of like the tenants that lived there. If it wasn't the elevators acting up, the door buzzers were out of order. Things were really fucked up for the senior citizens who couldn't walk that well because they became hostages in their own buildings. The Housing Authority superintendents didn't live there so who cared.

When Cream finally made it to Tootsie's floor, he gladly noticed silence in the hallway. Inspecting his gun once more, he crept slowly across the corridor up to door 708 with his gun drawn and bandanna over the lower half of his face. Reaching for the doorknob he clamped down on his teeth, gently turning it as softly as possible, hoping no one was sitting in the living room. When he pushed the steel door open at a snail's pace, it sounded as if two people were arguing in the other room. As Cream moved in closer with his gun aimed in one hand and a shopping bag in the other, relaxation struck overhearing Tootsie moan.

"That's it baby! Work that thing! Plunge that

dick harder baby, *harder!* Oh my god that's it!" Tootsie hissed in ecstasy.

Cream almost revealed himself by laughing. His main man Warren Hawkins was fucking the shit out of Fat Jack's girlfriend Tootsie Jackson and everything was going according to plan.

Tootsie was this forty-something year old Star Jones look alike chick that worked for Jack as both his bag up person and mistress on the side. She was kind of out of shape if you ask Cream, but the clothes she wore along with the way that she shook her ass made a lot of guys still want to hit it. People thought Tootsie and Jack were married, for the simple reason that he brought her gifts and took her out to eat more than he did his actual wife. Jack's legal spouse was Warren's aunt.

Tootsie's apartment was not just Jack's little hideaway, it was also his drug lab and stash house. Every time Jack copped his little weight, he'd leave it with Tootsie and go seek out Elephant, an old time acquaintance who cooked up his shit. Being a well-known dope addict, Elephant was not so easy to locate. Usually he was who knows where shooting junk into his veins. He had swollen heroin addict hands that looked really nasty, in addition to open puss sores all over his arms and legs. Even though the poison Elephant dealt with had nothing to do with poison ivy, it still kept him scratching.

Jack and Elephant used to roll strong together in their early twenties, but the former all-star athlete turned into a dope fiend after blowing a full time scholarship to BSU, which could have stood for *Bull Shit University* anyway. Sometimes Jack spent hours trying to find this dude because there was no one else in the city that would manufacture cocaine into crack for a measly fifty dollars and a large pizza other than Elephant. He would probably do it for free, since Jack was the only person who would reminisce and testify about his past athletic ability.

As for Warren, he was Cream's shadow. You wouldn't see one without the other. These two wild niggas had been tight since the third grade and like many other young bucks coming up in the streets they became products of the environment. Following those that came before them, Cream and Warren learned all types of clever schemes to get over. During high school Warren became the big time womanizer that he still is today. Watching his father charm the ladies rubbed off and being that War was a handsome brother with a little roughness in his demeanor, high school girls as well as a few graduate students fought over him all the time.

This ego boost led Warren and his sexual dexterity into furthering his hustle of manipulating the feminine mind. Chicks that had access to major paper were the only ones he was interested in and after thrusting around in a honey's kitty kat like an erotic physical trainer, Warren would start gaming them with chief bullshit. They usually got addicted to his superfluous bedroom treatment and started coming out of the pockets soon after, as well as coming out of other places too, if you know what I mean.

Emanating seductive sentiments with sinister charm best illustrates how his father taught him. Juicing simple-minded females for all the loot he could get became second nature for Warren. Eventually some of the smart girls compared notes, catching on to his *modus operandi* then broke off the relationship like a stopped check. Some women didn't care at all if Warren was using them, because he made them popular and they were dumb strung out on his magic stick. Women always told Warren that he resembled the dude from Groove Theory, but he didn't think so. Warren had a lighter cinnamon complexion with the height of six-two and a 195-pound muscular frame. Certainly the girly gossip that he packed an enormous size dick spread like wild fire in school.

Cream on the other hand was a little darker than his a-alike and had more of a huskier type of build than Warren did. Cream was packing too, not as large as Warren, but he filled the ladies up nonetheless. War's sexual ruse influenced Cream to freak the ladies also as a means to gain extra doe in his school days. He had already mastered the Art of Clitoris licking at fourteen from watching his cousin's porno flicks. One learned technique was to spell out the entire alphabet in long circular motions with his tongue sliding in and out of every orifice of the girl's body as he massaged her tic-tac.

Cream had one sexy high school playmate in particular, frequently tingling and busting feminine juice like a squeezed ripe orange. Honey was in love with his stroke too, but had a thing for oral PAP smear exams. Going downtown paid off well that year because the Caribbean wildflower that he tongue lashed daily, hit him off with enough doe to purchase his first ride. Her family was involved in the weed business and they constantly gave her large amounts of cash that she didn't know what to do with. So why not spend it on her boyfriend who was Cream at the time.

Cream wasn't even trying to milk the girl like

that cause when truth be told, she was the first to ever give him head and he really felt her style and enjoyed being with her. Honey kept him laced in the latest footwear and fashions, so instead of spending his money on expensive gear and jewelry like Warren was doing, Cream saved the money she gave him and bought a used Q45 Infinity. It wasn't big dog compared to the paid out the ass cats getting money on the block, but back then for a schoolboy that didn't sell drugs, pushing a Q to high school was like driving a Bentley. You couldn't tell Cream and Warren that they weren't the hot shit as they drove past other students waiting for the school bus.

*Anyway back to the scheme*, following Warren's lead, the duo had been working a plan on Tootsie and Fat Jack for a minute now. Cream's task was to watch Jack run his daily routine, which consisted mostly of eating at soul food restaurants and drinking Heinekens in front of package stores, while Warren had the pleasure of working his own routine on Tootsie.

In the short time that Cream followed Jack around town, he learned a lot about him. For a person Jack's age involved in the drug business he thought he would have more street sense or at least be a sharp dresser, but Jack was a naive sloppy muthafucka' with zero class. Quiet as its kept, reputations are always overrated in the streets. Although if you let Jack tell it, he would probably say he was some sort of big time pimp, because he drove around in a Lincoln town car with tiger print seat covers and ate barbecue wings in between stoplights...please!

Tootsie even wondered why Jack's wife put up with him for so long. The only reason Tootsie put up with his greasy ass was for the simple fact that she had been gankin' him for big bucks since the first day that they met waiting in line at KFC. After she got Jack to pay for her bucket of dead birds and biscuits, the next thing you know she's in the kitchen bagging up for him. Regardless of how much product or how much time that it took to package his narcotics, Jack would have her bag the entire amount while he sat on the couch watching bootleg movies. Sometimes it took all day. As long as she could grab his dick in public and tweeze his penis during oral sex, Jack didn't give a shit if Tootsie cut her fingers or not chopping away at the rock.

Surely Tootsie skimmed the product and every time Jack fell asleep drunk in her apartment, she would go through his pockets peeling off Grant's and Benjamin's. Fat Jack was really foolish, but cheaper than anything else and ironically his cheap ways cost him more in the long run. Tootsie had swindled more money from her sugar daddy than an Enron executive and it wasn't hard to tell that his entire operation was amateur night. Now it was only a matter of time before his ass got pulled off stage like a bad act at the Apollo Theater. Even if Warren didn't plot to get 'em, someone else would've targeted his spot.

Warren had literally worked on Tootsie's ass for weeks. Every time he came over she wanted him to toss her salad. He hated it cause she was a little funky down there, but he did what grimy niggas do *the dirty work*. Tootsie officially met Warren in the Side Effect West, a small bar across town. He followed her in there one night taking a seat next to her at the bar. Tootsie felt him playing her close, but just thought that he was sweating her plump rump. She hadn't a clue that he was planning to fuck her out of her boyfriend's money and leave her ass hanging to dry. It wasn't personal, "It be's like that some times," which means the company you keep could bring on unanticipated heat when you play life as a game.

All Warren had to do was tap that ass once and it was a done deal. From the first time that he and Tootsie had sex up to now, she never stopped hounding him for more. Any time she could acquire away from Jack, she'd page Warren leaving demanding messages on his voice mail. After rocking her to sleep, Warren would sneak around the cluttered apartment looking for the stash. This went on for a couple days until he discovered product hidden in a laundry detergent box under the kitchen sink. He knew there would be a fresh supply up in there today, because before Tootsie paged him Fat Jack had just returned from a trip uptown.

Every two weeks Jack drove to Harlem somewhere around Amsterdam Avenue, to re-up on those goodies the local fiends craved and loved. Even for a part time sucker like Jack, it didn't take long to move the sparkling fish-scale cocaine he regularly transported across state lines.

"We got 30 minutes. I want it fast and hard. Bring my dick home!" was the message Tootsie left on Warren's pager as soon as Jack dropped off the coke and left.

Jack had been gone for twenty-five minutes now, so of course Tootsie took advantage of the situation. After she left the two-way message insisting Warren come lay some pipe right quick, he sat in the truck with Cream and Drench enlightening them with the exact location of everything. All Cream had to do was put the shit in a bag and bounce. Warren's job was to work his tongue and swivel them hips long enough to keep Tootsie occupied, while his partner crept through the apartment. It was Cream's idea to switch the cocaine with Arm & Hammer baking soda, so if Tootsie took a quick glance she would think everything was straight. Nine times out of ten she would get the blame for meddling with the drugs anyway, because Jack tasted his stuff on the spot. As long as he wasn't absolutely positive about what happened and who did it, there would be fewer problems to deal with.

Although Warren was just as trigger-happy, he stated that he only wanted to teach Jack a lesson for now by playing with his mind and money first, after Drench suggested that they should shoot his shit up instead of just robbing his ass when they sat in the car conniving. Cream believed that money and beef don't mix either.

In the twenty minutes that he was in the apartment, Warren was able to lift about $13,000 in bills of fifty's and hundred's. While Tootsie caught her breath, he traveled back and forth from the bedroom to the kitchen where Jack had money stuffed inside coffee cans then back to the bathroom where he crumbled bills into the wastebasket. There were some pills and another $2000 War had his eye on, but it was in the bedroom closet tucked away so he couldn't get to it that easily.

"Thirteen should get me goin' again, maybe I'll get the rest some other time" Warren thought all the while going back and forth from room to room in between orgasms.

The third trip to the bathroom is when he

phoned Cream as the signal to come upstairs. He unlocked the apartment door to make it easy for Cream to slide in and out like he continued to do with Tootsie in the bedroom. Cream made the switch then gathered the loot in a flash. He also grabbed one of the three scales that were on the counter and two Guinness Stout beers from the fridge. The triple beam was too large to hide, but the smaller digital scale easily fit into the bag.

Creeping to the exit inconspicuously, Cream peeked through the cracked bedroom door only to witness Tootsie in a pretzel position. Her legs were pinned to the sides of her head and Warren's ass muscles were indented dripping with sweat as he pumped at top speed. War caught his friend peeking into the mirror reflection and expressed a paltry look.

Just as Cream stepped out of the apartment into the hallway, locks began clicking next door. He sped things up trying not to be seen exiting Tootsie's apartment. Things could get hectic if he were to get caught red handed and all, so he reached for his gun again.

Cream froze as the door to apartment 707 opened. Before he turned to walk away, this cherubic face appeared keeping him in place. Dressed in her little boxer shorts and tank top, Ma'ati stood under the doorframe with both hands on her hips clearing her throat. Cream just stared, while the young woman strolled into the hallway wearing bootie socks with small balls on the heel.

Ma'ati stared back at Cream with the same funny look on her face like she knew him.

"*What in the hell is he doing here*?" She thought.

"Are you the one who's been making all that

noise in there?" Ma'ati asked, taunting afterward, "Ooh Ooh *right there baby*, don't stop oh!"

Cream glanced over her shoulder trying to get a better look into her apartment to make sure none of Jack's boys were up in there ready to split his wig.

"Not me" Cream hesitated, "I um, was looking for this other chick's apartment. She had told me to come by her crib and holla' but I ah, forgot what door." He fumbled his words sounding more suspicious than if he didn't say anything at all.

"What's her name?" Ma'ati asked, "I know a lot of people in the building and I probably can help you find the right door."

"Huh?" Cream hesitated again before coming up with a phony name, "what? Oh her name is Yorika. I doubt if you know her cause I think she just moved in."

Ma'ati was new to the building herself and was just being nosy. She kept both of her hands on her hips leaning to the side. She was trying to read upside down what store brand was printed on the shopping bag he held so apprehensively. It was obvious to her that Cream was lying.

"That's okay" she said, "You don't have to tell me. Can I at least see what kind of feet you bought?" Ma'ati pressed, becoming more investigative.

"You don't look like you're into women's clothes," she giggled into a laugh, as she walked toward the corridor window after Cream said the sneakers were for him.

Cream was confused about Ma'ati's laughter until he reminded himself that the bag he carried was a Lady Footlocker shopping bag. He walked over toward the snooping dime piece that was now looking out of the window bopping her head to the music blasting outside. Most of the windows in the hallway didn't have any glass in them, so it was easy to look downstairs through the safety bars.

"That system is knockin'!" Ma'ati stated, winding her waist with both hands in the air.

Cream just watched as she danced, noticing that Ma'ati's nipples were protruding, sensitive from the cool night air that flowed through the corridor. His mind went blank for a minute, since women that looked as good as she did without all of the glamour and glitz fascinated him. But if Cream and his sidekick Warren were to make it out of the building without someone catching a body he had better move it.

# Scene Three

**Marveling at the sight** of Ma'ati's perky breasts under the thin tank top she wore, Cream snapped out of his trance when Ma'ati casually snapped her fingers. He realized the music blasting from outside was the signal that Jack had returned. Cream suddenly grabbed Ma'ati's arm ending her tantric dance routine.

"Is he crazy?" She thought out loud. "Boy you better get your damn hands off me! You don't know me likc that," she hissed.

"I'm sorry yo I really am, but look, I know you don't know me that well, but I was hoping you could do me a really big favor...if you can't I'll understand."

Cream put his head down with a distressed look in his eye. The elevators were still out of order, so Jack's out of shape ass would have to use the stairs. Cream could easily walk up to the eighth floor, wait for Jack to exit on the seventh then walk back down without being seen. The problem was that he left his cell in the truck and had no way to alert Warren without knocking on Tootsie's door.

*"Got the nerve to ask me can I do favors, grabbin' my arm like he's crazy*" Ma'ati said to herself, like Cream wasn't standing in front of her.

She put her index fingers to the sides of her

temple, like she was a physic mind reader.

"Wait a minute I'm getting a signal" she laughed, "it's telling me that you need to alert someone about something. Hold on I'm getting more...Tootsie's man is coming back and someone might get caught trickin' wit' her old behind."

Ma'ati moved her mouth close to Cream's face as if she was going to kiss him on the cheek, but instead she whispered softly in his ear.

"Fix your face son. You look silly with your mouth hanging open like that, I got you come on."

She led him by the wrist into her apartment before rushing into the bedroom, which was flush with Tootsie's wall. She pounded on the thin sheet rock creating a loud thumping noise. Whenever anyone banged on your wall in the projects, it meant you were either making too much noise or the police were coming.

Cream smiled admiring the way Ma'ati carried herself. She had a mysterious energy about her and anyone in her presence, even for a short period of time could tell that she was on point. She presented herself to Cream as sweet with a sprinkle of sassiness to keep him in check.

The music coming from Cream's truck could still be heard from outside. Ma'ati came back in the living room changing the words to the Blackmoon rap record, as she sang along with the backdrop music.

"Who got da' props, who got da' props, a five foot chick, who be blowin' up the spots."

Warren hurried out of Tootsie's crib with his shirt and jacket balled up in his hands. His jeans were unzipped with his belt dangling. He had one boot on, fighting with the other to get his foot all the way in. Tootsie slammed the door behind him, scurrying around spraying air freshener, since the whole place smelled like butt, funky pussy and cigarettes all in one odor.

Warren looked upset when he first spotted Cream leaning his head into the hallway from Ma'ati's apartment. Ultimately getting his boot completely on, he let out a Cheshire cat grin.

"Hurry up yo" Cream uttered, "Jack is on his way upstairs."

He took Warren's jacket from him while he caught his breath inside Ma'ati's apartment.

"What happened? You were supposed to call me when you left. Did you get the shit or what?"

Cream played like he fucked up, and then started grinning exactly like Warren did in the hallway.

"Aw man, I had you goin' for a minute, you know I handle mine kid" Cream replied, holding the shopping bag in the air for proof.

Ma'ati went back in her bedroom to change clothes. She poked her head through the door to speak.

"You're lucky I let you in here. I really don't know you cats like that, so I want both of you to clap your hands and keep them clapping until I finish gettin' dressed, ya' heard?"

"Who's that," Warren asked, "I think I seen her somewhere before?"

"Chill son that's me" Cream exclaimed, letting his boy know off the bat that he was interested in Ma'ati.

Cream was delighted that she was changing into something more appropriate now that Warren was in the picture. He thought that was so lady like.

"Stop clapping your hands, she thinks you

were trickin' with Tootsie, so relax and play along if she asks any questions," Cream spoke into a whisper as he told Warren how to play it.

Ma'ati appeared in the tiny living room wearing black sweat pants and a thin gray hooded shirt that had a faded picture of Assata Shakur on the front. She kept both hands inside the pocket of her pullover all the while standing like a soldier with legs spread three feet apart.

They thought Ma'ati was in her room just changing clothes, but what she was also doing was loading her small pearl handle .380. It was presently concealed in her pocket with her finger on the trigger. In her pants pocket was her blade.

"Let me introduce you to my nigga Warren," Cream proclaimed.

"What's really good precious" War interposed, "you can call me War, and your name is?"

"Tiara, but all my friends call me by my middle name Ma'ati. So I guess you can call me Tiara."

Cream cleared his throat officially introducing himself again.

"I'm Cream, nice to meet you Ma."

"The pleasure's all yours I'm sure" Ma'ati responded, fronting like she could care less.

"How do you pronounce your middle name, *my-yat-ee*?" Cream inquired.

"No it's pronounced like *Ma-aut-tea*."

Ma'ati took one hand out of her pocket, making hand gestures as if she could really speak sign language.

"What part of Ma'ati don't you understand," she slowly asked, in a deaf tone of voice.

"How 'bout I just call you Ma, is that ai'ight

wit' you?" Cream chuckled.

Ma'ati didn't answer him. She moved closer to the window looking into the parking lot, at the same time watching Warren from the corner of her eye.

"Didn't I tell y'all to keep clapping your hands? Where's my lighter?" She yelled, "it was on the table before you two came in!" Ma continued to shout.

Unsuccessful in her attempt to light a scented candle with an old pack of matches, Ma'ati used the stove flame. The reason she wanted them to clap their hands was if they stopped, she would know that their hands were doing something else, like stealing lighters maybe.

Cream and Warren both had a habit of taking people's lighters unconsciously. It was something they had picked up in the clubs. Pointing to each other with innocent looks on their faces Ma'ati got Warren first.

"I didn't know vegetarians smoked?" She said, leaving him to question her comment, as she walked into the kitchen.

War had a confused look on his face as if her statement was preposterous.

"Do I look like I'm into spoken word and veggie burgers?" He shouted back into the kitchen.

"Well since I heard you next door tossin' Tootsie's salad, I took an educated guess that you were a vegetarian, my bad," she laughed before taking a sip of juice from her cup.

"She got jokes, real funny," War said turning to look at Cream, "you should keep this one she's a real comedian and cute at that."

"He ain't keeping a damn thing, but his ass out of my apartment" Ma'ati rejoined, "both of you have been here too long as it is and I think it's time to bounce."

Fat Jack and Elephant had made their way upstairs ten minutes ago, so the coast was clear.

"Aw'right Ma, good lookin' out baby" War uttered, as he took the bag from Cream casually heading out the door.

Before Cream got up to leave, he realized while digging in his pocket for his keys that he had the lighter after all.

"See I knew it!" Ma snickered a giggle when he pulled it out, "You know what they say *if you steal you lie, and if you lie, you cheat*."

She snatched the lighter from him and Cream snatched it back just as fast. He then pulled out a wad of bills.

"First of all I'm not stealing from you, I'm buying the lighter." He handed her a fifty.

"Secondly, for doing me the favor that I asked, this is for you." He handed over the rest of the money in his fist.

Cream put his mouth close to Ma's ear like she did to him in the hallway. This time he got to whisper in her ear.

"You're beautiful, but you look silly right now with your mouth open like that, fix ya' face."

Ma'ati cracked a little smile fanning Cream with the money he just gave her. She enjoyed Cream's deep voice in her ear, and let him continue flirting a bit more before kicking him out.

"Why don't you put those shorts and tank top back on," he said, "especially since we're all alone again. Which by the way, most women don't do that for me. They keep walking around the house in the same ol' skimpy outfit like other niggas ain't around and shit."

Ma chuckled in awe of Cream's self-assurance, "Aw, how touching, you thought I changed my clothes just for you."

After tilting her head to the side to crack her neck, Ma took her hands out of her pocket exposing the pistol she was packing.

"Don't get ahead of yourself kiko, I was just doin' you a favor."

"That's cute, not as cute as you are, but cute" Cream said, staring into her eyes with a mischievous grin after Ma'ati cocked her pistol.

"That must be my cue to go huh?"

"I guess so," Ma answered back.

"*That is so sexy, she even has a gun*," he thought to himself holding in his excitement.

"Maybe I'll see you some other time?" Cream asked with thirst.

Ma'ati began closing her door slowly as Cream stood there waiting for an answer.

"Maybe you will?" She grinned, "anyway thanks for the doe, bye! __Clink!"

The hallway felt silent after the door shut in Cream's face. Even though they had just met, something definitely clicked between the two. Ma'ati was feeling Cream in the same manner he was feeling her, except she didn't show it.

# Scene Four

"**Purple bag over here!"** some cat shouted in the lobby as customers crowded the door.

Cream clinched his burner ready for whatever, skeptical of the clique blocking the exit.

"Make a line!" they shouted, "have your money ready cause this ain't that Cloud nine garbage."

"Right here yo, how many?" One of the workers motioned to Cream.

Cream looked at him without saying anything. The look on his face said it all.

"Get the fuck out of here with that bullshit," his expression hollered.

War was already in the truck bragging to Drench about the crazy sex positions he had Tootsie in.

"Man would you come on," War complained out the window anxious to leave. "Pussy brings you in this world and if you let it, pussy can take you out. Let's skate before you get us shot the fuck up."

Cream removed the burner from his waistband, before hopping in the driver's seat. War opened the two Guinness Stouts with his teeth, passing one to Cream and keeping one for himself.

Drench didn't need anything else to add to his spaced out behavior. He was still trying to hype the benefits of living in public housing.

"I'm with you D, I love the projects too," Warren blurted before downing his beer, "I don't know what the hell Cream is talkin' about?"

Even though Drench only stayed in the truck playing music, Cream hit him off with some cash like he promised. Stepping out the Yukon with a knot of twenties, Drench headed for the Chinese restaurant on the hill.

"Be safe man, get some rest too, you look terrible," War commented.

He wasn't lying. Drench sure did look bad. His eyes were blood shot, his hair needed braiding and he looked like he hadn't slept in days. As Drench walked halfway into the Chinese restaurant Warren called him back to the truck like something was dreadfully wrong.

"Yo I almost forgot to tell you, make sure you dip those cat wings in hot sauce before you chow down on that meow mix!"

Hysterical laughter roared from the Denali as Cream pulled off slowly.

"Hot sauce these nuts!" Drench hollered back.

He lost his appetite for Chinese food after the thought of fried putty cat and decided to hit the soul food spot next door, which wasn't any healthier.

"It looks like that fat fuck had damn near a kilo of raw up in this piece!" Warren stated, before smelling the blow.

He never seen a kilo in his life, so what did he know? Cream took his eyes off the road to quickly evaluate the amount of cocaine once more.

"Nah I doubt if that's a key, but that eleven thousand looks correct."

"Eleven!" Warren's posture shifted, "you mean thirteen right? I know I counted ninety one hundred dollar bills and eighty fifty dollar bills and the last time I checked that's thirteen thousand, so what'chu' talkin'?" he declared with mistrust.

"Nigga I just gave Drench some doe for watching the truck, you forgot? I gave Ma'ati some money too, cause she was the one that really looked out for us nah'mean?"

The whole robbery thing was to supposedly teach Jack a lesson for beating up Warren's aunt, but War was acting like it was all about the doe instead of reprisal.

"Why'd you hit D off anyway?" War ridiculed Cream's sympathy.

"You know how it is when a nigga's broke" Cream said, "Tania came up to us in the parkin' lot talkin' mad shit about how she wants money for their son or she's callin' child support on 'em. He really needed that shit, but you act like you're the one who's broke nigga what's the deal?"

Cream paused for a minute after Warren failed to respond.

"Besides, that shit came out of my pocket!" Cream added in response to his partner's misgivings, "so yeah there's thirteen in there now, but two is mine off the top, and you still owe me for the six hunit' you borrowed after losing all your money shootin' dice yesterday."

They sat parked in front of Warren's crib dividing up the money while conversing about Ma'ati.

"Damn, I can't believe you gave that chick a gee!" Warren let out, "I told you pussy could take you out, but it can also make a nigga broke!"

Before taking it in for the night, Warren asked Cream if he could persuade his uncle to break down the blow since he didn't know what he was doing. War supposedly had some white boys from out of town that were willing to pay high prices for crack, since drugs were not so readily available in their area. Cream listened intently and was skeptical of the whole idea. He was a hustler, but not a drug-dealer. Cream hustled the hustlers obtaining most of his cash from card games and sports bets. In any case he drove a nice whip and hung around the willies, so people still had him pegged as a drug dealer anyway.

In contrast Warren dabbled in every and anything involving getting paid, from playing women with good credit to dipping into the profitable drug business here and there. Sometimes he even dealt with stolen cars.

"I hope you're not schemin' on Jack's little block, cause they about to raid the entire Garden. All them bodies turnin' up made shit real hot."

"I ain't tryna' take over nobody's block," War affirmed, "I'm just tryna' make some extra doe off those spoiled powder face mutha'fuckas. I always charge them double sometimes triple. We could make mad money outta' town I'm telling you! Niggas 'round the way already swear we movin' big time product, so why not get paid for real for real?"

"I'm lettin' you know right now. I'm not fuckin' around with this petty shit son. I won about seven gee's the other night playin' down & dirty blackjack and got plans of my own nah'mean? You just said yourself that heads be watching us like hawks, so what makes you think the police ain't doin' the same!"

Before his grandfather died last month, Cream promised him that he would invest the money he accumulated gambling into something more productive. Cream's grandfather was wise and tried to school him about the politricks of the game. He noticed that the property value in Bridgeport was at a record low and predicted real estate conglomerates will soon move in. After they buy up all the gentrified property, you can expect the mill rate to rise. When this happens, Grandpa warned, "you can guarantee hustling will downsize cause there's no need for the State to let drugs flourish anymore."

Despite the reflection of his grandfather's insight, Cream got tired of Warren squawking about his dwindling finances and agreed one last time.

"Yo I'll see if he can do it tonight, but if not, that's that. I'm only lookin' out for you cause you my nigga" Cream declared.

"Ai'ight if he does it, come scoop me in the morning I'll be up" Warren affirmed.

As Cream turned up the music about to head home, he gave War dap before breaking off for the night.

# Scene Five

**On the other side of Bridgeport**, the streets always watched with scrutiny. The East End was predominantly black and the heads over there did not play games at all when it came to getting their money on. Hustling was a 24-7 operation. The entire area had become crime infested over the years and just about everyone outside day or night was involved in the drug trade one way or another.

Of course these things could not go down so smoothly if the police weren't involved somehow. Po-Po came through the block constantly shaking down niggas that didn't pay the "protection fee" they implemented or came around just to break balls. For a modest $2000 a week any drug dealer could rent out a corner to hustle on, even if they had warrants or beef with rival dealers that they also protected. This imposed security could include tips on specific raids to clemency on a body if you paid them enough. The police motto was to *Protect and Serve*, which most of them did very well...they protected the highest paying drug dealers and served warrants to the one's who didn't pay.

Cream had lived on the East End for years now, but grew up on the North End like Warren. The North End was basically a white neighborhood that surrounded a housing project along with a few black owned co-ops nearby. You couldn't find a white person on the East End, unless they were some kind of addict, a trick or the police.

Cream's mother Drusilla sent him to stay with his aunt Simone and uncle Raymond during his freshman year of high school. She thought it would be a good idea if he stayed with them for a little while, after her son got into a shoot-out with some out-of-towner's where they lived. What had actually took place was Cream was showing off his first gun one day, a snub nose .38 and it accidentally fired in the direction of some New Haven niggas that were parked across the street from him talking to a couple of girls.

While pulling off in a panic the New Haven cats fired back. Everybody exaggerated the story when they told Cream's mother that he had a wild gun battle and that was all Drusilla needed to hear. She had no idea that transferring her son to the East End was like moving him away from a campfire, seating him next to an inferno. Cream was 22 now and that was seven years ago. Luckily he didn't go down in flames.

Cruising down Stratford Avenue, which everyone commonly called *the Ave*, Cream spotted his uncle staggering out of the local pool hall with a small paper bag in his hand. He pulled along side of him screaming out the window like a fool.

"Run that shit old man! Hurry up, give me that drink or I'm gonna' let you have it!"

Uncle Ray stuck his hand in his coat like he was holding heat but he wasn't.

"Stop frontin' like you got a burner on you man, I know what a finger in the pocket looks like"

Cream laughed.

Ray held his chest pretending he was having heart trouble. He collapsed attempting to pick up the beer can that he dropped. Cream thought he was really having a heart attack and franticly jumped out the truck to help. When he did, Ray spun his nephew around into a headlock.

"Oh how the tables turn," he laughed.

They gathered their composure before getting back in the Yukon, each tired from the humorous tussle. Cream and Ray got along more like brothers, rather than uncle and nephew. They joked and cursed with each other all the time cause they were cool like that.

"Don't you ever pull a gun on anyone if you're not going to use it" Ray scolded, "I taught you better than that and what's wrong with you hootin' and hollerin' like you crazy?" Ray exclaimed waiting for an explanation.

"I got a lil' proposition for you if you're interested?" Cream said, "only thing is I need you to do it tonight."

"If I'm getting paid, hell yeah. I just lost four hundred back there playing black jack with those fools, so you right on time."

On occasion Cream would bring some of his close friends by to see Ray and he would cook up their little grams for a small fee. Unlike Elephant, Ray didn't use hard drugs, but he did drink most of the time. The only time Ray had cocaine in his possession was when it came to drug configurations.

"I hope you're not dirty" Ray huffed, "cause there goes TNT pulling over in front of Bert's. They just raided a minute ago and they better not pull us over or that's my ass!"

Uncle Ray was paranoid looking all around him, after Cream mentioned that the blow was hidden under his seat. The unmarked cars sped off passing right by them.

"Why don't you take another sip of that nasty ass Budweiser and relax. My shit is legit and there's no reason for TNT to be thinking about us."

Ray said he was more worried about his wife getting on him than he was worried about the police. It was the second time this month that he lost his entire paycheck drinking and gambling.

Waiting at the long light, Cream thought about a place they could use for a little while. Ray had him pull over by a payphone before they did anything else so he could call his wife. Cream offered his cell, but Ray declined. He said aunt Simone would recognize the number on the caller I.D and start asking a ton of questions.

"I'll just tell her I'm still in the pool hall gambling and that I might be a little late, because I'm winning lots of money," Ray disclosed.

Next stop was Vera's crib, a West Indian woman who Cream was sexing on the regular. With two children and an ex-husband who was getting deported very soon, Vera made sure she kept a man in her life. Cream slept at her place time to time whenever he wasn't sleeping over some other woman's house. Although in the last two weeks he'd only been by twice. Vera was getting sick and tired of getting dolled up, only to be stood up.

Cream figured since her rude boy ex-husband was getting deported shortly, Vera could use some extra cash and just might let him use her kitchen as a laboratory. He forgot she had a first-rate job and practically lived at the credit union. She had her own money and didn't need

Cream or her ex to support her financially. What Vera did need was love and affection. For some reason she attracted thugs and always ended up with heartbreaker bad boy types.

Vera lived all the way down the Ave. near the Bridgeport/Stratford Town line. Much older than Cream, about fourteen years older, her mature body was still off the hook even after having two children. Sexually their relationship was sweltering, but mentally Vera and Cream were on two different planets. At first Cream was rather pussy whipped, being that she constantly put it on him. After getting to know her more he learned Vera was looking for a long-term relationship that wasn't going to happen and knew eventually she would demand more out of their fickle relationship and kick him to the curb.

As soon as they pulled up to the house, uncle Ray opened the door ready to go inside.

"Slow down Unk, let me make sure everything is straight first. Just wait here for a minute," Cream instructed.

Ray lit a cigarette, sinking back into the butter soft leather. Walking up the squeaky wooden steps, Cream pulled out the house key Vera gave him. A light came on in seconds before he could completely insert it. Vera opened the door looking exotic as usual dressed in a violet silk night robe. Her hair was in a crisp French roll, like it was photographed from one of those black hair magazines. Manicure and pedicure of course. She stood there with her arms crossed revealing a hint of residual anger from the last time he showed up late. Vera cut Cream off before he spoke a word.

"Ssshh...the kid's sleep, me figure ya' come by late."

Her accent was as thick as her body and sometimes Cream couldn't understand what the hell she was saying, more so when she became angry but it sounded sexy to him nevertheless. Vera led Cream by the wrist into the living room where they kissed for a couple of minutes. She started to feel on his crotch something serious. Earlier this afternoon Cream boasted on the phone that he was going to blow her back out in the bedroom, talking about he was going to do this and do that. Vera forgot about being mad and was ready to hold him against his braggadocios sex talk.

"Wait, wait baby. I would love to splash it down right here in the living room, but I need to ask you something first."

Even though he was horny as hell, Cream wanted to take care of Business.

"What ting's a 'gwan?" Vera asked, getting upset again.

"You know I don't like to bring my dirt around you or your seeds, but..."

Vera cut Cream off with the "what is it now" face.

"I need you to be the darling that you are" Cream continued, "and let me use your kitchen for a little while. I promise I won't wake the kids."

She knew exactly what he was getting at because her ex used to carelessly manufacture drugs in their last house. Usually whatever Cream asked Vera to do she would go along with anyway, but he wanted to respect her by asking first. By not acting pussy whipped he actually got her to do whatever he wanted. It's called reversed psychology.

"Memba' me tell ya' bout bandulu

bizness...keep a play gangsta' and not know who dem a deal wit, ya' muss wan' end up in a dungeon."

"Vera listen baby, it ain't like that," Cream pressed, "his dumb ass was making sales out the front door. I just need to use the stove for a little while. It's nothing major. I got my uncle outside and he's gonna' do everything...you wont even know that he's here, I swear."

Vera rolled her eyes real extra, sucking her teeth additionally hard. She bumped Cream as she moved past him headed toward the entrance. Her luscious butt cakes were clinging to her silk robe, jiggling as she walked to the door. She turned around shooting Cream dirty looks every which way.

"I wan' nuff respect for me an my lickle youth dem, ya' 'ear" Vera said, "nun a dis' romp round all night, then wan' sleep ova' mess!"

"*Damn*" Cream thought, "*I knew I should've stopped by Rhonda's crib instead*."

He just knew Vera was going to kick him out, until she waved her hand out the door for Ray to come inside. Vera let them know from the jump that this would be the first and last time anyone used her kitchen for anything other than cooking food. She said if the police happen to rush in like they did once before, she's not flushing a damn thing or lying about shit either. Cream tried to clear the air by at least introducing Ray before he turned Vera's kitchen into a lab. Instead he talked to the hand as Vera's stop sign mushed his face before she walked out the room.

"Boy is you crazy?" Ray snapped, "you snatching shit like I owe you somethin'. Whatever problems you got with you and your woman, are your fuckin' problems, not mine. Don't make me whip your ass up in this woman's house nephew!"

Aggressively Unk snatched the bag back, throwing it on the kitchen table. He had to put his nephew in check. Except for playing around with his relatives, Ray didn't take shit from nobody. He drank and all that, but Ray could still fight his ass off and beat you down in a heartbeat.

"I couldn't understand half of what your lady was saying back there" Ray commented, "but I know when somebody's getting cursed out! Get used to it cause when you piss women off they have a tendency to do that."

"Lets just get this shit over with," Cream grumbled, "I don't wanna' hear her mouth all goddamn night,"

Ray changed the subject talking about some movie he watched last night. He started doing what he does, while explaining the benefits of ether. After breaking up the small powdered rocks, uncle Ray figured there was about 150 grams of cocaine on the table, which was far from Warren's novice assessment. Ray was old school and felt that he didn't need a scale. That was all good, but Cream wanted him to use Jack's digital to prove his estimation was on point anyway.

"Five ounces is a lot of shit to cook in the short time we're working with here. I'll tell you what, I'll cook half now and the rest later, aw'right?"

"Whatever man" Cream dully responded, "I really don't care right now, it ain't my shit anyway."

He left his uncle alone to go see what Vera was doing. She was sitting in the living room sipping on some coconut water watching a Sex in the City repeat. When Cream walked in the room Vera acted like he was invisible. She didn't say a word. She turned off the lamp and walked into her bedroom at the end of the hall. Seconds later Cream followed, closing the door behind him.

Vera's bedroom smelled blazing like Frankincense & Myrrh oil had been burning. Cream took a deep breath inhaling the aroma and before she could tell him off again, he pushed her down on the bed staring with a lustful glare. She lay there playfully on her back looking sexy as she wanna' be, turned on by his aggressive behavior. At a leisurely pace Cream took off his shirts, throwing them both on the floor. Vera undid her robe the same, gripping her breasts. She stared him in the eye as she licked her own nipples.

By now Cream was harder than a roll of quarters and needed to unravel some change. Vera kept exploring herself some more, spreading her wetness with one hand as she inserted her free hand's fingers inside. She tasted the sweetness off each finger one by one. More turned on than ever, Cream tested his patience continuing to stare at her thick puckered lips demonstrating their suction ability. After throwing on a Beres Hammond CD Cream finally joined in. He began licking Vera's chocolate kiss looking ta-ta's into melt down, at the same time massaging her clitoris in a circular motion.

Vera forcefully removed Cream's jeans and boxer's in a simultaneous manner. She grabbed his French bread, easing it inside her sexual oven. Moaning with pleasure, Vera bit into Cream's shoulder as he sucked on her neck thrusting away. About twenty strokes later she pushed him off her. Cream stood up with his rock diesel penis looking her in the face.

"What's wrong?" He growled, "You had me feeling so good why'd you stop?"

Vera didn't answer. She sat on the edge of the bed gripping his dick with both hands, sucking him off like crazy. The way she was going at it caused suction sounds to occur with streaks of saliva dribbling onto the carpet. The head was mind-blowing especially since this was the first time Vera had done anything like this to him, but Cream wanted the real wetness and couldn't wait. He pushed down on her inner thighs, spreading her honey well wide open, driving his dick inside with deep thrusts. After 15 minutes of solid revolving strokes they came one after another falling asleep.

# Scene Six

***It was now 4:00 A.M.*** Cream quietly put on his jeans and Timb's, tip toeing out the room into the kitchen. There he noticed a few yellowish discs sitting on the table. Uncle Ray had finished what he said he would do and was taking a nap. Ray was in the living room sleep with a lit Newport between his fingers, seconds from burning the rug. When Cream tried waking him before it happened, Ray jumped up ready to fight.

"Chill chill, it's just me man you were dreaming. Come on let's go I'll take you home."

Still a little groggy from his nap, Ray questioned his nephew's certainty that he was only dreaming.

"That Cadillac sure looked real...and those legs my god!"

Before they left, Cream covered the product with a towel after wrapping it in panty hose so it would dry faster.

"Aw shit, it's four o' clock!"

"Ssshhs! You gonna' wake her kids" Cream whispered.

"Why didn't you wake me sooner? Your aunt is gon' kill me," Ray whispered back.

The next thing Cream covered was the money his uncle lost gambling. He handed over $400 although Warren kicked up $300 for his time.

"Thank you very much, it's always a pleasure" Ray professionally responded.

Since his keys were somewhere on the dresser, Cream decided to take Vera's car. As soon as they got in the car Ray started.

"I know you're doing your thing, but you better be careful. Just cause you're fucking somebody don't mean you can trust them with everything."

Uncle Ray felt some concern about his know-it-all nephew's nonchalant attitude.

"There might not be pounds of coke on the table, but not for nothing, I seen guys get killed for much less than that. Just watch your back that's all I'm saying."

"True, but I'm not worried about Vera though cause she don't get down like that," Cream added.

Ray just frowned folding some money into his sock before getting out of the car.

"A man should have three pockets two for his wife and one for his self."

After stashing fifty bucks, he made sure that he had his house keys then tapped fists with his nephew before jogging up the steps.

"Be cool."

"Ai'ight Unk, peace."

Cream pulled off catching green lights all the way down the Ave. He was back to Vera's crib in no time, smoothly sliding into her nice warm bed.

The next morning, Vera was in the kitchen humming a tune while she poured batter in the frying pan. Cream wasn't up just yet, but woke soon after he smelled the nauseating odor of bacon sizzling.

"Distant lova... lova, lova..." Vera sang.

She immediately turned her attention to

Cream as she felt him sneaking up behind her. He gave Vera a kiss before jumping in the shower.

"Wa'sup bay-bay."

"You!" Cream asked walking away, "What's with the pork? You know I can't stand that smell."

Vera was in a playful mood this morning, dancing and singing along with the clock radio on the kitchen counter. She kept messing with her young luv as he showered, bringing about a cold surge with each flush of the toilet.

"Stop playing!" he yelled, "just wait Vera you're gonna' get it when I get out!"

With only a towel wrapped around his waist, Cream ran up behind Vera pinching her butt exceedingly hard as retribution for enduring the chilling shower. Vera laughed as he dropped an ice cube down her shirt escaping the clutches of her grasp.

She hollered from the kitchen as Cream ran into the other room, "Ya' hungry?"

"If you're serving more of you I am," Cream replied, "if not, I guess I'll have some of those other things," referring to the flapjacks as an alternative to Vera's own curvaceous tasty cakes.

Change clothes and go, was how it was in the mornings. Cream always had an extra outfit at Vera's, because whatever he would wear the last time he stayed over, she would wash and hang in her closet. Mulling over the few articles of clothing, he decided to wear his green and white football jersey, jeans and work boots. After getting dressed he snuck up behind Vera again, but this time to surprise her with a wet lick of the neck.

"By the way, I'm really sorry for leaving my shit on the table last night. I was dead tired" Cream apologized.

He grabbed a piece of toast Vera did not intend on sharing before he looked through the fridge.

"Where did you put that stuff by the way?" He asked with little suspicion.

"Top shelf in me closet" Vera rejoined holding her forehead, "if me pikny was to find it *oh lawd* talk 'bout furious!"

Vera acted tough, but was truly a sweetheart and Cream knew it. He always said to himself that if he was a little older and if she wanted to have more children, he would make her his wife in a second. On the other hand, since they were on such different levels mentally it probably wouldn't work out.

Like any other morning before school in Vera's residence, uproar came out of the living room.

"Mommy! Mommy! Shawn won't let me play with his Playstation!" a cute little voice cried.

Vera yelled back to her children who were playing video games in the living room just as loud.

"Please Shawn! Let ya' sista' play and come finish ya' food."

Shawn stormed in the kitchen pouting because his little sister always got her way.

"What's up lil' man you giving mommy a hard time today?" Cream posed, as the tyke grimaced at his food.

Vera pushed her son's seat in then straightened out Cream's green and white doo rag, going over her day's agenda. It was almost the end of the school year and both of her children were going on class trips. Shawn was scheduled to go to the aquarium and Nene was to hit the Soul Circus.

Vera said she was one of the chaperones and complained about her car being too small to pack in six children.

"No problem bay, you can use my truck. I owe you anyway for hittin' me off last night" Cream smiled, "you know what, I didn't expect you to do that."

Vera punched him in his arm like he said something wrong. She thought he was referring to her premiere oral sex performance last night.

"I wasn't talking about that!" Cream chuckled, "I was talking about letting me use the kitchen."

Vera stuck her hand in the trash then pulled out a crusty crack residue coffeepot like it was a dirty diaper. Cream offered to pay for a new one, but she turned down the cash, scooting her son away from the table.

"What'chu mean blood money? All money is blood money. Do you know how expensive the Circus is? Take the money and buy the kids anything they want," Cream insisted.

Vera rolled her eyes neatly folding the $200 into her bra. If she had been scheming like his uncle believed, she wouldn't have reminded him about the coffee pot in the first place. Opposite of what Ray had thought, Vera was honest and could care less about some stupid drug paraphernalia.

After ten minutes of play fighting with Shawn and tickling little Nene half to death, Cream got up off the carpet ready to leave.

"Bay you ready? I gotta' go."

She took her sweet time getting dressed then finally came outside to see Cream off. They shared a tight hug rocking back and forth. Cream stuck his head out of the window before backing out in Vera's Lexus.

"Have fun, and call me if you need anything. I'll see you tonight" he said, as Vera waved him off.

She knew that she wouldn't see him until late tonight because every time Cream drove her car he seemed to disappear. She scurried back in the house to answer the phone before Nene picked it up.

"'Ello?" She answered.

"May I speak to Ms. Edwards please?" A strange voice inquired.

"This is she."

"Muah!" Cream sounded, making kissing noises over the phone.

"I just wanted to see you run up the steps one more time and say bye again. You know I love watching your stuff jiggle, but I forgot to tell you the face to my radio is under the seat. Easy on the curbs cause I just got those rims. I'm out for real this time *one!*"

# Scene Seven

**9:30 a.m.** and of course Warren wasn't up yet. He was never ready when Cream came to pick him up in the morning. So instead of going straight to Warren's, he decided to waste some time hitting blocks. After burning enough gas fronting in the black Lexus Sport Coupe, Cream whipped it to the North End.

"*Sorry...is-all-that-you-can-say*" blared from the speakers.

Cream thought the disc he selected was Foxy Brown the rap artist, but oh well it was the reggae singer. Vera was generally into old school dancehall and besides a few other discs in the car that's all she really listened to. Certainly her speaker system wasn't as loud as Cream's, but it sounded nice and clear.

To Cream's surprise he spotted Ma'ati walking to the corner store as he made a right turn out of the Garden projects. Trying to be cool with his eyes off the road, he ended up hitting the brakes hard to avoid a rear end collision with the van in front of him. The Lex veered left screeching to a halt. Cream leaned over to the passenger side as the tinted window came down.

"Don't I know you?" He asked, "Maybe you can help me find this magnetic beauty I felt so attracted to last night. I left my heart with her, and hopefully she didn't throw it away."

Ma'ati smiled, walking toward the car. "Was that what that was?" She answered back, "I knew I smelled something rotten this morning"

"So what's the deal Ma, you need a ride or something? You're standing there like I got all day to flatter you," Cream flirted, with a handsome smile.

He acted like he had somewhere to go, but he was hoping that Ma'ati got in with him.

"Why, are you offering me a ride?" She gently voiced.

"Sure, that's the least I can do" Cream grinned, "Get in Ma."

Ma'ati got in, waving bye to whoever it was she knew at the bus stop. Immediately she smoothed her hands across the leather interior and started tapping on the wood grain with her red black & green French tipped nails.

"Hmmm? This is nice. Is this yours?" she asked.

Cream never responded.

"Wow you sure move fast" Ma'ati put forward, "that coke must have sold itself!"

Cream almost choked on the orange juice he was sipping. He jerked the wheel again pulling into the parking lot on the hill. The old time drinking buddies standing out there had to hop out of the way to escape a bumper ride.

"What the fuck did you say?" Cream queried.

"Don't you curse at me muthafucka'! I told you before, you don't know me like that," Ma went off.

"Pardon me Ma'ati, but what cocaine are you talking about?" Cream asked sarcastically being polite.

"You know what I'm talking about you used me, don't act stupid now, *pardon me what cocaine are you talking about,*" Ma'ati mimicked.

"I used you? How?" Cream pressed.

"You probably stole this car too I bet, that's why you didn't answer me."

"Listen Ma, calm down and start from the beginning please."

"In the beginning was the word and...."

"Will you stop! I'm tired of your damn sarcasm!" He yelled.

Ma'ati started to push all Cream's buttons to agitate the situation. She looked him in the face then bust out laughing.

"AWW man, I knew it!" Ma kept laughing, "if I didn't know it then, I know it now, cause your face just gave it away for sure. Don't worry yo, I didn't tell nobody nothin'."

"Okay detective," Cream inhaled a deep breath, "what makes you think for some strange reason, I stole something from somebody."

"The something is blow and that somebody is Fat Jack! Act like you know. About ten minutes after you left last night, all types of shit started flying! Jack sounded pissed off. He got real loud then started throwing bottles at the wall. Somebody messed up bad, cause I heard some dude scream out 'It wasn't me! It wasn't me!' then POW! A shot went off. 'Where's my shit!' POW! I was standing in the hallway then closed my door cause I didn't want to be an innocent bystander know what I'm sayin'...POW! Another shot went off. Tootsie ran out into the hallway screaming like Jack was ready to kill her. She knocked on my door like she was crazy, but I took too long to open the door

I guess, so she ran into Tee Tee's crib two doors down. Her dumb ass called the police and got everybody knocked. Jack got arrested, the dude he shot and Tootsie."

Ma'ati told the entire story in one breath, it seemed.

"Okay I heard all that," Cream huffed, "so how do you figure I fit into this?"

"I was born at night, but not last night! Obviously you and your boy set Tootsie up. Come on, you acted all silly in the hallway about the bag you were holding" Ma'ati sucked her teeth, "then you give me a thousand dollars? You didn't know I was watching you from my window the whole time you were parked in your truck. I didn't know if you were federal agents or what. You never know who's lookin' for you these days."

"Ai'ight Ma I'll give it to you, you're observant, so now what?"

"What? You're giving me a ride ain't you?"

Cream pulled off in a hurry eager to tell Warren the news.

"Where you going anyway?" he asked. "I can drop you off right quick then swing back and do what I gotta' do."

Ma'ati smacked her juicy lips together causing a loud pucker.

"Well first, I need to get a money order, then I was gonna' hop on the train, but since you're driving, you can take me to Brooklyn."

"Brooklyn! I know you don't expect me to drive you out to Brooklyn today?" Cream frowned, "you must be buggin'."

"Why not?" She asked, "you say Brooklyn like it's poison."

*"If I take Vera's car to Brooklyn she's going*

*to have a fit!*" Cream thought, "*but Ma sure is looking good right now! And I wouldn't mind parlaying with her sexy ass in the city.*"

"I'd love to let you front me off as your boyfriend today," Cream reacted, "but right now I got a lot of thing's going on nah'mean? How 'bout tomorrow?"

"Oh its like that kid? That's okay, pull over right here!" Ma blared.

She mumbled under her breath, "Shady ass niggas for real. Let me out right here! I said stop the fuckin' car!"

Usually Ma'ati didn't curse unless she was excited or upset, but when she did, her Brooklyn girl accent became even more prominent. She was mad that Cream was acting funny over a ride, especially since she let him into her crib last night.

"*Well she did look out for a nigga and that would be fucked up if I diss her over a ride,*" Cream reflected.

He kept on driving, ignoring Ma'ati's demands to pull over. When they stopped at a light Cream put his hand on her shoulder as she attempted to get out in the middle of traffic.

"How 'bout this Ma, as soon as I politic with War on a few things, I'll jump on 95 and we'll hit Brooklyn in less than an hour, cool?"

"Don't do me any favors" She coldly responded.

"You looked out for me, now let me return the favor. It's only a ride."

Ma'ati gave a super fake smile unfolding her arms.

"You don't have to apologize," she emphasized, "just don't curse at me again cause it disrupts balance."

Cream dialed Warren's home phone number once more. This time it picked up on the first ring instead of the answering machine activating.

"Yo who this is?" someone answered.

In the background War could be heard yelling at his little brother for answering his phone.

"What did I tell you about touchin' my shit!" he yelled, snatching the phone away.

"Yo who this is?" he answered the same as his brother.

"Who it sound like punk?" Cream retorted, "I told you I was coming to get you nigga, hurry up and get dressed I got some shit to tell you."

"Tell me now."

"Man, just get dressed."

Warren wouldn't let Cream hang up so easily without reaching for answers.

"Don't tell me you fucked one of the twins we met at Club Carib?"

Cream switched his cell to the other side of his ear. He looked over at Ma'ati making sure that she wasn't all in his mouth.

"Man you late! I wrapped that shit up the next day."

"Word? You never told me."

"Just come outside I'm out front" Cream laughed.

"Click!"

While parked in front of Warren's mother's house, Cream showered Ma'ati with flattering comments on how nice she looked. Her hair was cut in layers and the fashionable jean suit she wore was hugging her home wrecker curves something severe. Ma'ati let out a genuine smile this time as the comments kept coming.

"I'm serious you really look cute today...not

to say that you didn't look cute yesterday either" said Cream, working a dose of charm.

"I told you Cream you don't have to apologize or sweet talk me, but thank you anyway."

Ma continued thumbing through Vera's CD collection while Cream looked her over. She wasn't just a Brooklyn cutie with attitude; she was the epitome of beauty period. Ma'ati was petite from the waist up, but from the waist down she had that thickness that drove men crazy! Juicy like a Veryfine fruit drink, her apple bottom was beyond rotund resembling two halves of a basketball attached to her lower back. She may well have been related to the lovely African woman Saartjie Baartman *Venus Hottentot*.

With track star thighs and hand size breasts that curved upward, Ma'ati was definitely stupefying. The small birthmark under her left eye only enhanced her otherwise impeccable rich caramel complexion. No one could doubt Ma'ati's physical beauty. However it was her magnetic aura that really absorbed Cream's attention. Still reading the back of a Capleton CD, Ma could feel Cream checking her out and decided to entice his curiosity. She removed her Jean jacket to give him a better look.

"If you don't mind me asking, are you Jamaican?" Ma asked folding her jacket in her lap, "Black is Black, but I notice that you're really into dancehall music."

Cream shook his head implying that he wasn't. For some reason he didn't want to say that the car was Vera's. Warren came out to the car at last, hyped up of course when he spotted Ma'ati sitting in the front.

"That's ok shorty, don't get out I'll sit in the back."

Warren acted like sitting in the front seat would make Ma'ati feel special, but she was like whatever.

"Can you stop at that corner store over there?" Ma requested, "I need to get some money orders."

Warren leaned over into the front seat after she got out the car.

"Dayum yo! She could stand a small child on that ass! You're lucky I didn't meet her first" War grinned.

"Why you gotta' talk about her like that?" Cream affirmed defensively, "It's not what you think. I saw her walking to the store before I came to get you. I'm just giving her a ride son."

"Yeah right, what did you have to tell me that's so important?" asked Warren, blowing off Cream's protective attitude.

"Jack got cuffed last night."

"Stop lying! How you know?" War responded with delight.

Cream fixed himself in his seat, repeating the story Ma'ati told him.

"He flipped out and shot Elephant after finding out his money was gone and his shit was fucked up...they took Tootsie's ass downtown too."

Ma'ati came back to the car in the middle of the conversation after waiting in line only to find out that the store didn't sell money orders.

"So what nigga, Tootsie ain't gon' say shit. Jack will really kill her, if he knew she had me up in the crib diggin' her out every night."

War stopped fussing with Cream then asked Ma'ati about the rest of the story.

"What else is there to tell you?" she said, "Jack shot somebody, Tootsie got scared, Tee Tee called the police, and they're all in lock-up. What else you need to know?"

"Do you know what kind a police got 'em or what they were charged with?"

Ma'ati made eye contact with Warren through the rear view, stating that she didn't know and wondered why he asked.

"If regular uniform cops ran up in the spot, they probably didn't search the house thoroughly. But if the DT's got 'em that shit is probably gone," Warren heaved a sigh.

"What's gone?" Cream asked, looking just as curious as Ma did.

"The other money Tootsie had stashed in her closet," War divulged "I couldn't get to it, so you know..."

He gloated that he was only able to obtain $13,000 of the cash squirreled away in Tootsie's apartment.

By the time Tee Tee called 911, officers responded to the incident as a domestic violence call. When the police arrived to the scene, they found packaging materials, a bleeding Elephant, Jack's gun, and a small amount of weed that Tootsie left on the kitchen counter along with a white glob of foaming mess.

Being that Cream switched almost all of the cocaine with baking soda, there wasn't enough in the large glass beaker for the drug charges to stick. Although, the gun and residue left on the counter was still enough to spend a few nights in North Avenue County jail.

"That ain't right" Ma reacted, "why'd you get that woman in all types of trouble like that. What did she do to you? Or do you just go around robbing all the women that you meet?" She snickered.

"I had beef with Jack over some personal matters," War explained disdainfully, "Tootsie happened to be my way of handling it," he said.

He demonstrated how Jack beat the shit out of his aunt during a spades game.

"Yo Jack got mad when he lost and took it out on my aunt. He slapped her twice then punched her in the face because he said it was her fault that another couple ran a Boston on him...if it wasn't for you Ma'ati, things wouldn't have gone so easily. I'm doin' all this for my aunt so I'll give you a third of the money if you let me chill in your crib again for a minute. I don't want to look so hot."

Cream thought his boy's proposal was silly. He couldn't figure out why Warren was so persistent on going back into Tootsie's hot crib for a couple of dollars. It wasn't making sense.

"Letting those crooked ass cops take the money so they can buy their fat wives chinchillas would be a waste now wouldn't it" War griped, "I'm telling you Cream, narcotics didn't even get the paperwork sent to their desk yet." he argued.

"Okay, we can stop by my spot for a minute" Ma'ati said, "but we can't stay too long cause I gotta' go somewhere, remember Cream?"

Cream thought for a long time reluctant to answer, he remembered that he had Warren's little drugs in the trunk and turned back around.

"Before we do anything" he said, "Warren's ass is gonna' drop this shit off at his spot cause I'm not driving through the Garden dirty."

Ma'ati was starting to suspect that what she had originally thought about them was wrong.

They acted more like petty thieves rather than the big time drug dealers everybody thought they were. Unbeknownst to Ma'ati and other people who clocked Cream's figures, the coke he and Warren swiped from Tootsie's apartment last night was the largest amount of drugs the two ever had in their possession. Supposedly it was to be the last of any amount for Cream, after he made it clear that he was ready to rise to the next level without the B.S. in his midst. Warren had other intentions.

# Scene Eight

**In the mornings exclusively,** Housing Authority had cornball security guards posted in the lobby. Small offices were built for them similar to the same offices prison guards use upstate, called "the bubble."

Ma'ati had them follow her lead entering the building.

"Don't sign in" she said, "just play along and say you're with me."

"I wonder why they got security in the morning and not at night? That's backwards If you ask me," Warren stated as he lit a cigarette.

"They try to make it look like they're doing something around here" Ma'ati jeered, "the older folks might buy that crap, but you know the deal with security...they don't care what goes on, they just want you to sign your name so they can get that little check."

"What could they do anyway, hit niggas with flashlights" Cream poked fun, "throw fuckin' keys at us!"

All three laughed walking passed the punk looking security guard as he tried to get them to sign in. Cream was about to take the stairs, but oddly enough the elevators were working this morning. An old lady was exiting the elevator carrying a bag of empty cans.

"Excuse me darlin' how we doin' this moanin'. You live on the seventh floor don't you honey?" the nosy lady asked, "I hope you weren't involved in all that mess up there last night?"

"No not me Miss Jackson," Ma'ati replied in an innocent voice, "I was minding my own business. You think I was tryina' get shot!"

Miss Jackson gave the guys however, a screw face look as they squeezed passed to get on the elevator.

"You boys staying out of trouble? Those jails are full of babies like you who made bad decisions."

Warren nodded his head like a little boy getting chastised as Miss Jackson talked to them as if she knew they were up to no good.

"There won't be none of you hard heads left if you keep it up," the frail elder voiced walking away.

"I think they turn these damn elevators off at night on purpose," Cream commented after the doors closed.

"The projects be on lockdown," he said, "like this is some sort of public housing prison. Walking up all those stairs at night is ridiculous!"

"I thought you knew!" Ma'ati interjected, "that's why they call it the PROJECTS. They're just that, a government science project. When ever I hear the word 'public' used I think of it as a code word that means black people, like public housing, public assistance, public healthcare, public transportation, and public schools. Everything that's PUBLIC is usually fucked up and seems to only have black people involved, except the public library!"

"That's interesting, who told you that?" War asked.

"Told me? Nobody has to tell me nothin' just take a look around you."

"I feel what you're saying, I just never hear that many sisters breaking it down like that, but please spare me the lecture" said War.

When they got to the seventh floor, they went right into Ma's apartment. Last night Cream hadn't taken notice of how neat and clean she kept her place. It was spotless and smelled like burnt sage all through the apartment. Ma'ati drew the shades, which immediately shone sunrays, spotlighting the books that were stacked on the entertainment center. She had way more books than she did CD's, other than most people who had just the opposite, but then again Ma'ati was not most people.

"Did you read all these books?" Cream shouted into the kitchen, while his prospective love interest washed her hands.

"Not yet," she hollered back over the noise of running water, "I just finished reading the *48 laws of power*, and I just started the thick one, *Blueprint for Black Power* its off the hook so far."

Cream was thinking, "*Damn it would probably take me three years to read this big ass shit.*"

Ma came back drinking some juice, smiling at the frown Cream had while holding the big black book in his hand.

"I'm sorry, would you like something to drink?" she asked.

"I'm good, thanks. I got some orange juice in the car," Cream replied.

"You know it's not really the size of the book

that's important, it's what's inside that counts and how it makes me feel" Ma flirted, before sipping her juice some more.

"What'chu think? Should I shoot off the lock or what? I'm ready to do this!" War blurted.

"You probably would try that!" Ma chuckled in awe of Warren's turbulent demeanor.

"If you push the door hard enough it should open," Ma said, "the police kicked it in last night so you should have no problem."

She was right, the door was busted and of course housing didn't fix it yet. War eased his way inside going straight to the bedroom. He fondled one of Tootsie's pillows and pulled out two large zip lock bags full of Oxycotin. He stuffed the pills in his crotch not forgetting the $2000 hid in the Goose down jacket hanging up in the closet.

Warren was in and out in one minute. He let himself fall back into Ma'ati's couch, spreading out some cash on the coffee table. He held a thin stack of bills in his hand like a butler holds a dinner tray. After reimbursing Cream for his gambling debt, War gave Ma her share of the money for doing next to nothing, then slid Cream his pistol back before they left.

It was almost noon and they bullshitted in the apartment long enough. Cream didn't tell Warren where he was taking Ma'ati until the last minute, because he would have wanted to roll with them. War could be a real cock-blocker sometimes, so the brother had to sit this one out.

"I promised shorty a ride and you know I live by my word, so I'll check you later son just watch ya' back out here."

"All day everyday!" Warren exclaimed.

During the ride to Brooklyn, Cream started making basic conversation with Ma'ati to pass the time.

"So tell me Ma, what brings you to Bridgeport?" he asked, "I mean it's obvious you're not from around my way."

"My Grandmother you could say. She lived here for years and I was back and forth between BK and Bridgeport most of my life. The rest of my family still lives in Brooklyn though, so I'm still goin' back and forth *ugghh*" Ma'ati sighed.

"Does she live in the Garden?" Cream went on to ask.

Ma looked as if he said something wrong.

"Well, grandma made her transition a few months ago. She had a heart attack after arguing with some young bucks that were selling in front of the house."

"I'm sorry to hear that," Cream replied solemnly. He had lost a grandparent also, and knew what it felt like.

"I don't mourn anymore cause I understand death. I know Grandma is partyin' wherever she's at, but anyway she lived on the East End."

"Say word! I live on the East, what street?"

"Originally she was from Father Panic Village, when it was still called Yellow Mill, but you know how things got hectic over there. So she moved over to Fifth Street which wasn't any better."

"Bloody Fifth?" Cream questioned.

"I don't know, is that what they call it now?"

Ma'ati shrugged her shoulders staring out the window like she wasn't interested in talking anymore.

Before there was a "bloody 5th Street" there was *Father Panic Village*, New England's first public housing project. Huge in its initial construction, it almost spanned half a square mile from Waterview Avenue all the way to Pembroke Street. During the early eighties as the drug game rolled in hard, "The Vill" for short, developed into a war zone. Everyday someone was found dead or wounded. Infants and young children were shot daily from the stray shots that idiots let pop off for no particular reason. Most times the cause for taking a life was over petty arguments involving drugs. Arguments turned into fights, fights turned into shoot-outs and you know the rest. R.I.P

In addition, some of Bridgeport's first crack millionaires came out of the Vill. It's not a reality to say that anyone who sells drugs becomes a millionaire, but since Bridgeport sits in Fairfield County, one of, if not the richest county in the country...niggas got paid! As a whole, rich white people with expensive habits surged the city with millions annually.

Practically every building in the Vill had something being sold out of it drugs or not. Perimeters were established and anyone who crossed those lines trying to make a sale got shot at or shot up. Cream's Uncle "Scoop," who is deceased now because of his occupation, told him once that he had to shoot some dude in the ass for being out of bounds, like he was some sort of street referee in a drug game.

Cream heard stories from elders all the time about how they used to leave their doors open at night in their day without anyone trying to tie them up or steal anything from them at all. The elders said everyone got along in the Vill and looked out for each other back in the day. That must have definitely been just in their generation, because in the 80's and 90's with all the crazy ass murderers on the prowl you were lucky if you made it to your door! Never mind leaving the shit open.

God forbid if you were injured or sick, cause your best bet was to drive yourself or get a ride to the hospital instead of calling an ambulance. Flavor Flav was not kidding about 911 being a joke. With all the shootings and other crazy shit that took place in the Vill daily, the ambulances as well as the Police stopped responding to most of the distress calls made from there. Squad cars were shot at frequently and run out like roaches as if the police were a rival gang. So I guess they got the hint to stay out. It took the State almost fifteen years to completely demolish the Village. There were about eight major housing projects in Bridgeport's history, but Father Panic Village was definitely the most infamous.

Ma'ati continued to stare out of the window lost in her thoughts. Arriving at the Whitestone Bridge, Cream gathered four singles to pay the ridiculous toll.

"What part of Brooklyn we headed to Peaches?" he asked, pulling Ma'ati out of her trance.

Since everybody called him Cream, he thought Peaches and Cream sounded good.

"Huh?" Ma asked getting it to together, "what did you say?"

"Which way?"

"My bad, hit the Grand Central Parkway east then switch to the Jackie Robinson," Ma'ati instructed.

Waiting at the Pennsylvania Avenue intersection Cream probed if everything was all right.

"Yeah I'm fine," she said, not sounding very convincing, "I was just thinking that's all, I'm okay."

It seemed like talking about Father Panic brought back painful memories for her or something, because her exuberant disposition quickly turned to a sullen mood. Cream was afraid to dig any further. Ma'ati didn't tell him that the reason she spent so much time between BK and Bridgeport was because a tragedy struck her when she was much younger, wherein she never truly recovered.

*One night when Ma'ati was 11 years old she slept peacefully curled up in her mother's bed. Everything seemed fine in the modest Bed-Stuy first floor apartment. Her father, Akoben, was coming home from a hard day's work like any other night but this night was strange. Making his way down Lewis Avenue he noticed that the living room window was left wide open with their long cotton floral drapes blowing outside in the wind. Garbage cans were stacked underneath the ledge with a crate on top.*

*Akoben became alarmed creeping up the staircase, at the same time reaching for his pistol, the same .380 that Ma'ati carries with her to this day. He always thought living on the first floor without bars attached to the windows was a dangerous idea, but at the time his wife didn't want her family to feel like they were prisoners in their own home.*

*Regardless of how either of them felt, crack heads and dope addicts were notorious for breaking into places basically stealing anything they could get their hands on. Just as Akoben put the key to the lock he heard a panicky clatter. He pushed his way into the apartment with his gun drawn, quickly firing three shots at the shadowy figure scrambling through the living room.*

*"Pop! Pop! Pop!" the small handgun sounded.*

*The desperate dope fiend dropped dead instantly. Ma'ati screamed, "Mommy! Mommy! Get up! Get up, what's wrong!"*

*When Akoben burst into the bedroom, there laid his wife bleeding on the floor holding her stomach. Her eyes were still open and she was slowly dying. Akoben blanked out like he was back in Vietnam. Ma'ati was hysterical too. She didn't know what was happening and why.*

*At the time that her father shot at the intruder, he hit the dope fiend twice, while the last shot went right through the bedroom door fatally striking his wife in the stomach as she got up to see what all the noise that woke her was about. Ma'ati watched her moms die in her father's arms and that tragic memory still lingers in her mind today.*

*To no one's surprise, the court system in New York was backwards and like anywhere else, justice was not served. Ma'ati's father was sentenced to ten years in prison, for involuntary manslaughter and aggravated assault. Even though the gun was never recovered, it had little bearing on the sentence. Ma'ati lost not one, but both parents who were only trying to protect their children.*

"Take a right on Junis, then pull into the second parking lot" Ma directed, as Cream hit the corner. She looked out the back window trying to see if she recognized any of the people crowded in front of the Big R grocery store across the street.

"I hope we don't have to walk too far cause

I gotta' go big time," complained Cream pulling into an empty space.

The orange juice he drank in the car started to run right through him and from the way he was squirming in his seat, Ma thought he was going to get out and do the pee-pee dance.

Spread out in front of the ten-story project building was another crowd of people, about 25 or more teenagers enjoying their half-day of school hanging out in the Vandyke Housing projects. Not even out of the car thirty seconds, kids started sitting on Vera's car. A cute little girl in ponytails brought her Double Dutch game to a stand still, to run over and greet Ma'ati.

"Tiara!" the little girl yelled excitedly, hugging Ma's legs, "I missed you."

"I missed you too pumpkin *Cream* this is my lil' cousin KeKe."

KeKe waived her hand wildly, jetting inside. Ma'ati's cheerful mood was restored and she seemed energized again. A couple of brothers' grilled Cream for a second then kept on doing their thing. Ma'ati pinched her nose getting on the elevator since it reeked of urine.

"I think that's so nasty!" She commented, "they probably live in the building and don't even think about their own mother or any one else that has to smell this stench."

Cream didn't share his thoughts, cause he used to be the type to break the lights and irrigate the elevators himself. He matured since then, but right now it didn't sound like a bad idea. Little Keke knew what time it was and that's why she took the stairs.

The rancid odor switched from stale urine to Chocolate Ty in a matter of seconds. Cream loved the way weed smelled burned in rolling paper because the smell reminded him of his youth when he played on the swings at Seaside Park back home. As they entered the apartment, they heard Keke almost blow the surprise visit.

"Guess whose here mommy? Guess!"

Ma walked in behind her little cousin before she could tell her mother who it was.

"Your favorite niece," Ma'ati revealed.

Ma's aunt was talking on the phone in the other room. Ready to explode, Cream asked Ma'ati where the bathroom was located.

"Down the hall to your left" she replied.

He dashed down the hall almost knocking the woman down as she came out to greet her niece.

"Excuse you *goddamn*!" Sherl fumed, "Make sure you lift up the seat, I got no time to be cleaning up nobody's damn mess! I have enough shit of my own to clean."

Sherl stood there yelling at Cream through the bathroom door. Ma'ati cut her aunt off from continuing.

"Hi! Sherl! Good afternoon, Sherl! Nice to see you too, Sherl."

"I'm sorry Tiara, what's up girl, you just don't know, that nigga can get on my last nerve!"

"Who, Cream?" Ma asked, totally bewildered.

"Cream? Who in the hell is Cream?" Sherl retorted, "I'm talking about Keke's father Evan. I just hung up on his cheap ass."

Cream jiggled the toilet handle to stop it from running. When he came out, he interrupted their conversation with an apology.

"I'm sorry miss, I didn't mean to move past you so fast, but I had to go, nah'mean. No disrespect misses... um?" Cream waited for a name.

"You make me sound old *Miss*? Call me Sherl. I'm Tiara's wonderful and sexy aunt. And don't worry about it, when you gotta' go, you got to go. Its nature honey...next time just go before you come!"

Cream sat down next to Ma'ati on the cracked leather sofa in front of a wide screen Gateway plasma television that was too large for the cramped space. Sherl began picking up all the toys lying around.

"What made you come by today out of all days?" Sherl asked, "out of all days that I didn't clean, you would bring someone with you."

That was Sherl's way of explaining the mess.

"I can't visit my family when I want to? I never see you anymore since I've moved to Connecticut," Ma'ati whined with attitude.

Sherl put one hand on her hip acting like Ma's complaint was silly. She was a big body girl with a cute face, small hands and small feet, but everything else was big. You could tell that Sherl didn't let her age or her children stop her from doing her thing by the way that she worked it.

"You act like I moved to west bubble fuck" Ma'ati sneered, "Bridgeport's less than an hour away and if I don't stop by once in awhile I'll never see you or the rest of the fam."

"Aw, come give me a hug. Its nothing personal you know that Tiara. Connecticut just doesn't do it for me. I got warrants up there plus the snobby rich people sipping tea and watching the Lifetime channel all day is not my thing."

For some reason people always thought that if you lived in CT, you were rich. Black people go through the same struggle no matter where they're living.

"I can still use a phone call or two, ya' know. Instead of urine in the elevators we got shit in the hallway in case you get homesick," Ma shot back.

She was being sarcastic cause Sherl was just making excuses for not visiting.

After Ma'ati got up to get herself a drink of water, Sherl put her niece on blast.

"Your mother taught you better manners than that" Sherl chastised, "ask the man if he would like something to drink too."

Sherl looked over at Cream, "would you care for a drink honey?"

"No thank you," Cream politely answered.

Ma giggled, "He damn near knocked you down trying to get in the bathroom to get rid of fluids, I think he's fine."

"*I think he's fine too*," Sherl mumbled under her breathe with flirtatious eyes.

She sat down next to Cream asking twenty-one questions.

"Are you married?"

"No not yet."

"Why not? You're a nice looking young man. You're not gay are you? Most of the good ones are gay, locked up, or married."

"Or like Evan," Ma cut in referring to Sherl's children's father.

"You ain't say nothin' wrong!" Sherl gave her niece a high five trying to hold in her laugh before she chuckled, "He sure is a lying ass cheap mutha' uh unt!"

She went on for ten minutes about how terrible men are these days. Cream stuck up for homeboy even though he didn't know him. He was just sick and tired of always hearing that all men are dog's bullshit.

"If all men are dogs," he said, "what does that make the women they come out of? Mothers tell their sons they're too young to be with just one girl. Explore the world they say, but those same women complain later about men who can't be with just one woman."

Cream didn't mean any disrespect, but why did he go there. Sherl was heated. She got her neck to moving, and her hand jus' a going.

"Nigga look here! I raised my son with respect. Any disrespect he picked up was from out there in the street or from that crap music you call rap music! Don't you tell me about unfaithful men or scandalous women!"

After a short conversation about cheaters and gold diggers, Cream left the issue alone. Ma'ati asked her aunt if she had heard from her sister Shell lately. Sherl whispered something back then they shared a serious look with each other. After they talked for another twenty minutes Ma'ati stood up ready to leave. Keke had gone back outside to play with her friends.

"Before I go I want to give you something. Here's a lil' cash to use on bills or the kids, I mean children," Ma'ati corrected herself.

She said the word kid means baby goat and that goats were known to be sacrifice animals.

"I think we sacrificed enough children in the streets already. Children or seeds are a better description to call our futures cause words have a lot of power and when you speak those words they manifest somewhere in the universe."

Sherl stood there with her arms folded.

"Ironically my niece became a philosopher after she dropped out of high school Cream. I can't believe she studies more now, than when she was actually in school."

Ma'ati's father would always mail her letters from prison with lists of books he wanted her to read. He told her that the only true education truly obtained, is the one you give yourself. Akoben was behind Ma all the way with her decision to leave school in the tenth grade.

Just like Cream and his uncle were cool, Sherl and Ma'ati shared that sister type of vibe. Ma'ati gave her aunt $2300, which was $200 short of all the money that she received for helping Cream and Warren with the Tootsie thing.

"Girl this is way too much money, I can't take this," Sherl said estimating how much it was, "I didn't even get a full check this week, there's no way I could repay you."

"It's not a loan don't sweat it. Now if you don't take this money I'ma beat you over the head with it" Ma'ati huffed, playfully attacking her aunt with her fist.

While the ladies talked finances, Cream looked over all the pictures that were hanging on the living room wall. One in particular caught his attention leaving him to stare.

"Isn't she beautiful?" Sherl stated softly.

The woman in the picture looked divine, like an older version of Ma'ati.

"That's my big sister, Tiara's mother. I swear she sounds just like her mother talking all that philosophy stuff."

Ma put her jacket on, smiling with watery eyes.

"She passed on," Sherl added, "but I can tell they share the same spirit."

The room got quiet. Cream wondered how

her mother died, but didn't ask. Ma'ati had gone outside for a minute to look for Keke downstairs as well as wipe her tears away.

Moments later Ma'ati snapped at Laquan who was sitting with some friends in the stairwell.

"Don't even look at me!"

"Its still all about you sweetness. I just want you to know that baby girl. What up can I call you?" Laquan pleaded.

He knew Ma'ati moved to Connecticut and just wanted to hit it again.

"Who's that nigga I seen you go upstairs with?" Laquan asked like he wanted beef, "he betta' not be ya boyfriend cause sons in my hood now with my girl...he can get touched nah'mean Tiara?"

"Yeah, you mean you ain't gonna' do shit! Get out my face Laquan," Ma retorted.

After no sign of Keke and bumping into her ex in the lobby, she went back upstairs.

"Now don't go spending all that money on weed Sherl, we smelled that skunk burning when we first came in" Ma'ati jeered as she re-entered.

"I bet you did. I'm a grown ass woman Tiara let me handle mines...allow me to tell you Cream, Tiara and her friends used to smoke more reefer than Redman and Method guy," Sherl laughed, "matter of fact they taught me how to roll a blunt."

Ma'ati laughed along with her aunt waving away the cigarette smoke that she blew in her face.

"That's right!" she said, "and I quit been there done that, next! And for your information old lady, it's Method *man* not *guy* So there!"

Halfway out the door they hugged, expressing how much they loved each other. Sherl gave Cream a hug too. She even told him that he could stop by any time that he wanted, with or without her niece. Sherl was just playing, but she did have that flirtatious energy.

"Seriously Cream, keep her out of trouble and you better not get her in none either or I'll be up in Connecticut looking for you with my golf club" Sherl testified, as she walked them to the elevator.

She must have repeated how cute they looked together seven times. Cream embellished the compliment by putting his arm around Ma'ati's neck like they were taking pictures.

"Tell your father I asked about him when you visit and please tell Keke to get her butt back upstairs if you see her," Sherl asked before the elevator door closed.

When they got outside Cream spotted KeKe running from some little boy. Ma'ati hopped Laquan was still around so she could flaunt Cream in his face, but he was gone. After Ma'ati told KeKe that her mother was taking them to Chucky Cheese the little cutie took off running.

"Wait! Where's my kiss," Ma yelled out. KeKe ran back out of breath giving her cousin a quick hug and a kiss then took off again.

"Have fun kay. I love you KeKe."

# Scene Nine

**"Get your ass off my car!"** Cream hollered, irritated that some children were jumping on the roof of Vera's Lexus like it was a trampoline.

"I'll get down when I feel like it punk!" the young boy with fuzzy cornrows shouted back, before jumping down and running off with his friends.

Across the parking lot were the same grimy looking group of cats that were chillin' with Laquan. They looked like they had been scheming on Vera's coupe, since the tags were out of state. Cream pulled off slow, spitting phlegm out the window while reflecting the same hard looks they were throwing his way.

"Keep startin' trouble. Those niggas over there are old school Decepticon's and won't think twice about shooting up the car with us in it."

"That's why I got my..." Cream felt for his burner.

"Where's my shit?" He distressfully asked himself.

"Chill killa', I got it right here," Ma handed him the gun.

"How'd it get over there Ma'ati?" Cream animatedly asked, "If they started popping off, were you gon' clap back? No! I didn't think so."

"For your information buddy I'm a good shot" Ma said, "You'll be okay Rambro, just breathe and exhale. *Breath exhale and relax*."

Ma'ati was having a ball clownin', but Cream was getting vexed. Between the countless dollar vans and other vehicles double-parking out of nowhere, he kept getting stuck in traffic. Some guy was half out the car talking to another who had his head sticking out the sunroof.

"Come on man! What the fuck! Lets go!" Cream yelled at the Arab driving the gypsy cab.

He was suddenly blocked in because a car behind him stopped close and the cars on the drivers' side sped past.

"You in a rush? Chill sun just breathe and exhale, let me stop playin' before you crash. Just stay in the left lane."

Cream gave his hilarious passenger a dirty look.

"You can't be ready to bounce," Ma'ati playfully whined, "cause I didn't get to front you off as my man like you promised boo."

"Oh I'm your boo now?" Cream smiled at her mockery.

Flanked by badass kids jumping up and down on the car, on top of staring contests with rabble-rousers and terrible foreign drivers in Brooklyn, Cream lost his cool for a second. Now that Ma'ati seemed to desire his company some more, he quickly regained his smooth composure. He didn't even know himself why he was so upset because he double-parked and stared at out-of-towners all the time.

"I'm a let you in on somethin' sweets. We don't have to act like we're a couple" Cream murmured, moving his eyebrows up and down, "we can make it happen nah' I'm sayin'?"

After Ma'ati pinched his cheek, Cream stated that he was starving and asked if she knew of any nice spots to hit. While they cruised down Halsey Avenue, Ma'ati turned her attention to someone that she must have known. She damn near broke her neck looking back frowning. It was Laquan posted up with some thick chick, although ten minutes ago he was begging Ma'ati to take him back.

"Anyway, let me see..." she pondered, biting her lip.

"I heard a lot about Mars twenty-one twelve or how about Puffy's joint?" Cream mentioned, throwing out suggestions.

"I was thinkin' something a bit more private" Ma said, "but if you don't mind crossing the bridge I know a spot."

She broke it down to two places. It was going to be either Emily's or the Uptown Juice Bar, which were both in Harlem. She enlighten Cream that the Juice Bar had blazing vegetables and the rest of the food was off the chain too, but that Emily's was more of a first date type of spot.

"I don't care, I just wanna' lounge and relax" Cream smiled rubbing his stomach, "so being our first date and all, Emily's it is."

When they got to the nice and cozy restaurant it was just starting to fill in. Cream chose a window seat quickly pulling out Ma's chair for her. He wasn't really the gentleman type, but doing so gave him a better look from behind.

"*Oh my god*" Cream mumbled to himself.

"What'chu say," Ma'ati asked, not quite hearing what he said.

He simply shook his head implying

everything was okay. The exceedingly pricey Manolo Blahniks field boots that Ma'ati had on, made her succulent cheeks stick out even farther than they normally did. Cream had the same expression as that little white boy Macaulay Caulkin from the movie *Home Alone* when he held his hands to his face in shock.

An extra gentle gentleman came over placing two complimentary pieces of cornbread on the table while they were being seated. The gay waiter grinned at Cream as he caught him admiring Ma's celestial sphere. Cream screw-faced the waiter causing him to bobble his tray of tea lights. Ma'ati kept wondering what Cream was smiling at so damn much.

"Its just nice being with you" he commented, "you're so...I'm lost for words. So, so right for me."

Ma'ati truly had it poppin'. She was the type of female any man would wife up and one thing for sure, was Cream never felt his breathing flutter in the midst of any other woman. He just thought she was *the most beautifullest' thing in the world.*

Ma'ati was flattered but played it modest. While looking over the menu, she started saying something about a book that she was reading, but Cream wasn't really paying attention cause he was still revering in his thoughts about sex.

"They say the secret to a healthy diet is to never eat anything that has a mouth or a voice?"

"Can I ask you a question Ma, are you a Muslim? You always seem to mention books or something that you've read. I'm just curious?"

Ma'ati didn't let Cream's dense assumption get to her. Many people had the tendency to presume she was some type of religious fanatic, even though she hardly ever mentioned the

Q'uran, Holy Bible or any other religious idioms.

"Why do people always classify a black person to be Muslim as soon as they hear them talking about life's issues? No I'm not a Muslim, but I can't understand why people ask me that just cause they hear a sister speak her mind or whateva'?"

Ma fixed her sleeves neatly and kept on talking.

"Tell me something Cream, how is life for you in the street day to day?"

Cream took a sip of water before responding to the question.

"You know it's razor hectic out here. Every day's a battle."

"Okay then, well in warfare you have to prepare, like studying your opponent for starters. If you don't examine the plans of your adversary, how can you make informed alliances? You need to know the specifics of those you do battle with in order to maneuver and contend."

Cream was like whoa! He was besieged in Ma'ati's perception of the daily grind and warfare. It was true, people these days didn't seem to study anything around them except each other's cars and clothes. Maybe since there were so many distractions in life they didn't have the time to observe and enjoy it. Creativity was extinct and only a few realized that they've become mentally frozen, merely reactionaries to latest news headlines.

Another waiter stood at the table asking them if they were ready to order.

"How yeww doin'!" He asked, sounding just like the Wendy Williams sound effect. He stood there eyes wide open, twitching side to side as he waited for them to order.

Ma ordered for herself while Cream was still looking over the menu.

"I'll have the vegetable platter and a lemon zinger tea for now, thank you" Ma smiled.

Cream handed both menus back finally deciding what he would have.

"Okay I'm gonna' have the sautéed salmon with buttered spinach and let me see...a Guinness stout bottled, no draft shit though ai'ight?"

He took another sip of water continuing the conversation.

"Son is two snaps up, did you peep those tight ass spandex slacks?" He displayed a look of shame rather than disgust.

"Yeah I know, it's an epidemic these days. More and more brothers are turning to homosexuality rather than deal with the stress of being a black man. It throws everything off balance when a woman has to step up to take the role of daddy."

"Carpet munching and dookie love is their business," Cream joked, "but what kills me is that gay people just want everybody to know their sexual affairs...what's next, flags for those who like to do it doggy-style, flags for missionary position lovers, flags for people who like to do it standing up..."

"I get the point, sexual preference has nothing to do with racism, but they make it look like being gay in America is like being Black in America. And what's the definition of a Homo-thug?" Ma'ati laughed at her own thought,

"The system don't perceive gay brothers as a threat in the corporate world, they even promote that shit and more than likely hire them just for being gay! I'm beginning to think there's homosexual mind control goin' on. Next time you're in a bookstore, peep how the African-American section is always right next to the Gay and Lesbian section. It's like that in every major bookstore that I been in. Coincidence?"

Ma'ati was talking with Cream like she was in a beauty parlor chatting with her girls.

"Take a good look at any housing project. They're specifically designed for women to play both parental roles and I'm not even going to get into how feminized boys become after mama has to raise them by herself. It's like the State has taken place of the father. If the daddy's around, forget about section eight cause they'll cut your ass off like that" she snapped her fingers,

"And if his stupid ass gets knocked for some dumb shit, then we're left for dead trying to survive by our damn selves. *Is it all fair in love and war*?" Ma questioned.

Cream interposed on Sherl's situation given that they had a similar conversation over her house.

"I'm not sticking up for every nigga who does his women wrong, but most of us are just trying to make it know'what'm'sayin'. Sherl seemed content to me," Cream stated.

"Please! Auntie gets WIC, rental assistance and all other types of dependency programs. You can't see how she could despise her children's father for not being responsible?"

"Trust me, Sherl don't want no part of that Bull, but she has to, just to keep a roof over her head and feed her children. Evan needs to stop being a *baby daddy* and step up as an *adult father*."

Ma'ati was blowing off steam for her aunt and women period, but at the same time she was trying to explain to Cream why a lot of women felt the way that they did. Many sisters were trapped under dependency programs like state assistance and rather than blow away like grains of sand in a windstorm, they stood strong doing the best they could do.

"I'm telling you yo, the State treats sisters like slave making factories. Our babies come out of us as state property. You could say the hospital is the auction block and the birth certificate is the bill of sale."

After Ma'ati finished dropping science, Cream did the knowledge from his perspective.

"I'm one of those niggas tryna' make it and for most people that means do what you gotta' do to survive. For others when you move outta' your hood into a white hood, that's 'making it'. But then if everybody tries to make it, we'll all jus' be trying to escape from each other. I realized makin' it was inside here," he said as he tapped his finger on his head then his chest.

Ma'ati sipped her tea interested to hear more. The Guinness seemed to have Cream on the talkative side, but he was nowhere near drunk. He just felt comfortable talking with Ma'ati. He paused for a moment lost in thought, then downed the rest of his beer going on to explain how some album he heard the other day mentally threw him.

"It was some shit about hunting wolves in the Arctic. When they hunt a wolf in the Arctic it said they put blood on a double-edged sword then stick it in the ice so the blade is sticking out. When the wolf walks by, he smells the blood thinking he's about to eat, so he licks the blood from the blade, but as he licks the blade he cuts his tongue and keeps on licking. The wolf thinks he's licking something else's blood, but he's actually feeding off his own. Obviously he bleeds to death...but yo that's exactly what happened to niggas in the drug game, everybody got their turn to eat off their own, then died off."

Cream and Ma'ati shared one of the best conversations dealing with life and love that they've had in a long time. Sometimes Cream would tell Vera how he felt about things, but the response that he got back was empty, whereas Ma'ati was more on his level. During their meal the two pragmatists learned that they had a lot in common. They both seemed to endure the gusts of ignorance that swept through the hood.

"I'm glad you gave me a ride today Raheem. I really enjoyed spending the day with you" Ma acknowledged, while gripping Creams wrist.

Cream paid the bill and also left two tips for the waiter. One tip was $15 and the other tip was a comment, in which Cream told the waiter that tight pants cause testicular cancer.

# Scene Ten

**Cream and Ma'ati** were both feeling relaxed and comfortable with each other. Comparable to when you meet a person for the first time and you felt like you've known them all your life. It was about 9:00 P.M. and Cream had just realized that he spent the entire day with Ma. Earlier this afternoon he turned off his cell. When he checked his messages in the bathroom at the restaurant, he learned that Vera had called seven times so far. He suspected that she was probably bugging about the car.

It was all about Ma'ati now. Cream didn't think about Vera all day until he checked his messages. Ma'ati slipped in an Alice Coltrane CD that she had in her purse before they hit the Bruckner Expressway. For almost the whole ride neither one said two words to each other. There was no bad energy or anything they just let the music play cruising in deep thought. Ma'ati was laid back in her seat chillin'. Cream floated in the Lex switching lanes with the smoothness. The instrumental work of art played at mid volume as they headed back to Bridgeport. Cream was imagining being with Ma intimately and how things would be if she were his girl. Ma'ati had this look as if she was high, but she wasn't. Her eyes were closed zoning to the music.

Out of the blue Cream pulled over into the I-95 breakdown lane not to far from a rest stop. Ma'ati opened her eyes to see what was happening, and to her surprise Cream leaned over and started kissing on those soft juicy lips of hers. She looked at him like he was crazy at first, but was also smitten for the moment.

"Crea...?"

Before Ma'ati could get out the rest of Cream's name, he kissed her again. This time with one of his hands holding the back of her neck and a lot of wet tongue added. They sat there making out passionately like high school kids as vehicles passed by at 70 mph. This spurt of infatuation went on until a State trooper pulled behind them flashing his lights. The officer came over to the passenger side tapping on the window with his flashlight.

"Is there a problem here ma'am'?

"No we're okay officer," Ma responded, "we just had to pull over so we wouldn't overheat."

They both started laughing at how innocent they felt kissing each other. After shining a light in Cream's face the trooper got back in his cruiser taking in that his services were not needed. Surprisingly he didn't even ask them for I.D or registration.

"See I told you, black people can't even kiss without the police fuckin' with us!" They both laughed.

10:30 P.M they were back at Ma'ati's building. Cream decided to walk her up to her door, but before they even got to the entrance a teenage kid army suited down, ran up to him asking questions like he knew him.

"Sup Yo? How many bundles did you bring for us? It's flockin' out here, tell War that Dwayne ran out already so we'll probably need some more. Why you looking at me like that, you gonna' hit us off with work or not," the kid badgered, as Ma'ati walked away.

"What the hell you talkin' 'bout cuzint!" Cream shouted, "don't ever fuckin' run up on me like that again! I'll hit you off with something all right," he said as he lifted up his shirt gripping his pistol. "I don't even know you son, so get the fuck out my face!"

Cream was pissed. His burner was fully displayed now and the nervous halfway thug got the message. He placed his palms forward backing away, hoping that Cream didn't shoot em'.

"My bad B, I'm runnin' low and War said he would send out some more work, so I just thought..."

"Don't think," Cream said walking away, "that's your problem. *Ma'ati wait up!*" He shouted.

Cream walked away in the middle of the kid's apology. He jogged to the building trying to catch up to Ma'ati who was already walking up the stairs. He noticed that Ma'ati seemed upset cause she wasn't saying anything. Something really pissed her off.

"So I guess all that shit you were saying over dinner was all a front, huh?"

"What?" Cream looked confused.

"I can't believe it. How stupid of me to think you were any different from the rest of the blood suckers out here. I can't believe you!" Her voice rose.

She paused for a minute, and then continued to stomp up the staircase.

"I should've known that you were trying to use me. You must think I'm like Tootsie's dumb ass don't you?"

Cream tried to keep up with Ma'ati as her boot heels clicked faster and faster up the stairs. He tripped crossing in front of her.

"Hold on baby, hold up, you got it all wrong let's talk for a minute."

"Talk about what BROTHA'! We already did that and I can see you try to run game on a chick."

"It ain't even like that," Cream pursued, "I thought I let you know that I don't wanna' play games with you?"

Ma'ati nervously fidgeted her keys into the lock as her eyes were getting glassy.

"Tryna set up shop like I'm some...psshhsshh," she thought out loud, exhaling a gasping breath.

Finally opening the door she turned around to look at Cream.

"Remember when you were telling me about wolves in the Arctic?" Cream sluggishly nodded yes, "and how they hunt them and shit? ...Well let me tell you about the fox in the city. The fox is sly. His mannerisms are a little different than the wolf and he approaches his prey circling and grinning, but what you find out about the fox when it's too late, is that the wolf and the fox have the same appetite!"

Ma'ati slammed the door in Creams face so hard that it made an echo in the hallway that sounded like gunfire. Cream jumped back stunned.

"My thoughts were genuine. I wasn't actin' or tryna' play you" he yelled through the door, "I'm not a fox or a wolf. Open this door right now and let me talk to you."

Cream leaned on the door pleading for about 15 minutes with no success. Like many other women, Ma'ati had been in situations time and time again where men lied attempting to use her to get whatever they wanted. Most of Ma'ati's relationships were with thugs who thought they had crazy game only to find out she was two steps ahead of them. Her assumption that Cream was trying to play her had a lot to do with the way in which they met.

Ma'ati was by no means naive to the drug game or how niggas got down to come up. She figured Cream was trying to set up shop from her apartment like Fat Jack had done with Tootsie. Cream and Warren's little heist had takeover written all over it, plus homeboy downstairs made it appear like they were already handing out packages. Actually Cream knew nothing about the things Warren had going on.

When he got off the elevator downstairs, the same crew of young cats with some more anxious wanna' be's, crowded the lobby. They all used to work for Jack, but since Jack was in county jail and couldn't make the bail, the project youngster's were starving.

"*Yo there he goes,* my man, you holla' at ya' boy yet?" One of them asked Cream, "Cloud Nine is tripling over there and we're tryna' get paid too what's up?"

"Didn't you hear what I said before" Cream roared, "get the fuck out my face! Move! Get out the way!"

Cream pushed the biggest one out the crew knocking him to the floor. After snapping on everybody else's ass, he peeled out in Vera's car vexed. Up until now Cream never gave a rat's ass what any women thought about him, except his mother and aunt. He could care less and move on to the next, but for some strange reason he felt like he owed Ma'ati something. Talking with her made him think about his future.

Waiting at a green light Cream deliberated on where Warren could be since he wasn't home or answering his cell.

*"I know where his stupid ass is," he thought, "the Snake Pit..."*

Realizing that he'd been waiting at a green light as if it was red, Cream ran the light almost causing a collision.

Unless there were a fire or a murder the night before, street level drug dealers to old time willies gambled at the Snake Pit. The Pit was this run down pool hall on the East End of Bridgeport, where all types of shady shit took place. They sold drinks after hours and played music so it was really like a little club that rarely closed.

It was there at the Snake Pit where Cream made most of his money. Not from selling drugs or whatever, but from gambling. Apart from the money and perks that foolish women gave up, it was War's main source of income too, but he couldn't count cards as well as his boy could and eventually drifted off into other schemes, like playing the drug dealer role.

Cream took total advantage of silly entrepreneurs who would stand on the block getting drunk all day, while they hustled drugs. Sometimes he would even encourage their habits, like casinos do when they pass around the tray of free drinks to loosen you up to gamble. In between liquor swigs and smoking a few blunts the mood was finally set for a card game.

Around midnight before the third shift took over the grind, the suckers who hustled all day foolishly getting drunk, gambled their hard-earned money into sober minded pockets. Any shrewd individual could see how easy it was to finagle intoxicated niggas money away. Some people do dope and some smoke crack, at the same time some dealers get drunk and smoke weed. Still and all, one person's indulgence is another person's bread and butter.

It takes a fool to lose twice and most of the fools that gambled every night lost almost every night. Would you believe the lowest level worker, the one who risked his life and freedom daily, actually sold $1000 worth of crack (g-packs) for the sorry profit of $100. They then turned in the other $900 to the lieutenant. Nevertheless those same clowns laid big bets on the table with their little 10%. A few clever cats moonlighted on the block double dipping, whereas they would sell two different brands of product, but the only thing was if they got caught it was lights out.

Cream had the whole "hustle the hustlers" thing, down to a science. By midnight he could count on at least five drunk niggas fronting like they were paid, dropping a minimum of $250 to $300 a piece just bullshitting around shooting dice. The big money however was in playing Black Jack.

When a person loses their money fast like in a dice game, they're sometimes reluctant to continue doing so. But a card game seems to prolong the process of losing and encourages dummies to play longer. Some didn't mind losing because they still got props for being a big spender. I guess the illusion was more important than the paper.

There was equal opportunity in the Pit on Thursday and Friday nights. The place would be crowded with 9 to 5 cats that sniffed or drank half of their paychecks, betting the rest away. One could make $1500 to $2000 a night easy. No transactions or armed robberies, just straight gambling, which isn't too shabby for a couple of hour's playing cards. The only thing was that the Snake Pit was a magnet for stick up kids and heedless shootouts. Everyone in there with any sense kept a burner in their waistband or had back up laying in the cut. It was definitely a dangerous place to hangout.

Street reputations played a big part in how long a person lasted without getting tested. Warren had an ill rep for blasting heat first, and asking questions later. So this of course carried over for Cream who had acquired the nickname for winning big boy cash all the time and knocking niggas out for ass betting. When Cream pulled up to the spot he parked right across the street from the underworld after hours casino. Like any other night mad heads stood out front blocking the entrance.

"*Cash Rules Everything Around Me, my nigga Cream gets the money*!" Bing-O announced as Cream got out the car.

"What's the deal god? Show a nigga some love," he shouted, "I jus' hit the brick yesterday!"

Cream hip-hop hugged Omar welcoming him home. Everybody called Omar Bing-O, because he practically did his entire prison sentence in solitary confinement, a.k.a. "the bing." Bing-O must have done push-ups all day everyday cause he was huge now. He was grizzly before, but with a new bulk muscular physique and an old short temper, he was even more treacherous than before he went in.

"I see you're still doing it Cream your coupe is sitting pretty over there god."

"Nah that shit ain't mine," Cream confessed, "I'm jus' drivin' it, but what's the deal son, you straight?"

Cream turned around for a second watching his back as cars rolled bye. White boy Geek walked up behind him and stood next to Bing-O then pulled out a bottle from his back pocket like he was reaching for a gun. Cream eyed his every move keeping in mind his relationship with Jack. He didn't trust anybody on the Ave as it was. After Geek started drinking, Cream eased up and continued conversation with Bing.

"Yo, you don't even know son, me and this nigga right here go back like spinal cords," Cream raved, "this is one of the craziest niggas in Bridgeport!"

He hit Bing-O off with a few Benjamin's since he just got out the box.

"Here yo, take these and cop you some new feet. Use this twenty and get you some black shea butter soap cause I know that Lisa prison soap was eatin' you up!" Cream laughed.

"Good looking out god, I'ma see you."

Now that Bing-O was back on the brick, Cream knew it was only a matter of time before people started getting robbed again up in the Snake Pit, cause Bing-O was crazy enough to stick-up the stick-up kids and didn't care who he shot. He wasn't studying the 120 lessons in prison it was just a front so people would think that he changed.

Thick cigarette and weed smoke filled the air in the pit and music was playing, but the people gambling were much louder than the old ass jukebox.

"Usually I only give bitches my number!" Warren yelled, "so write this down y'all, four fifty six on yo ass!"

War was holding a fist full of twenties and collecting some more after rolling C-low on the crowd that hovered over the dice. Cream made his way over to the table with just about everyone acknowledging his presence.

"You're just in time my nigga," War grinned ear to ear, "Wanna' go half on a black jack bank? Cause these chumps can't shoot no dice."

Cream didn't look as happy as his boy, while War continued to heckle the crowd. He grew agitated the more War joked.

"Look at this clown with glasses, he can see low, but he can't roll a c-low."

War snapped his fingers as he rolled the dice again.

"Uuhh! You see it, fuck you pay me! Head crack! Pay as you play or get ya' head cracked!"

Cream had to slow War's roll. He wanted to talk to him about the little incident at building nine.

"Let me talk to you for a minute," Cream affirmed.

He put his arm around War walking him away from the game.

"Explain why niggas in the Garden act like you run a block. They even think I work for you. Niggas ran up on me for packages and I almost popped one of them silly ass kids," Cream stressed.

War stepped back to see what was going on at the table, while Cream waited for an answer.

"It's still my bank so put those dice down,"

he yelled toward the table then looked Cream in the eye.

"I don't know what you're talking about."

"Makin' moves and moving bundles out of Ma's building is what I'm talkin' about?" Cream replied angrily.

"Who told you that?" War laughed.

Cream briefly went into how he was approached on some bullshit, which blew up his spot with Ma'ati.

"I was about to smack fire out a niggas ass cause Ma got pissed at me like I was co-signing your scheme. She thinks I'm running game on her like...tryna' set up shop in her building."

War started laughing again, "was my little brother with them? He swears he's somebody's lieutenant. He probably took some of the product that I left in my dresser. I bet you he's out there with his corny friends tryna' hustle."

Cream wasn't amused. He got loud with War, suspicious that he was lying.

"That sounds like some bullshit to me, I know you son, you're trying to take over building nine," Cream voiced loudly.

War didn't like anyone yelling at him period and that meant Cream included. He looked around making sure no one was paying attention to Cream tearing into him. The gamblers were anxious to start a new game, so Warren took Cream out back so they could talk privately. Only regulars and ghetto superstars were allowed to go out the back or come in that way, because it led to a dark alley and was the perfect get away or entry for a robbery.

"Don't talk to me like I'm some fuckin' herb ass nigga Cream. People might get the wrong idea and think I'm soft or some shit and then I'll have to shoot a muthafucka'" Warren retorted.

"Don't play that gangsta' shit wit' me nigga! You know I ain't the one."

Cream refused to let War snap back at him, but listened to what he had to say. Warren leaned on a garbage can looking down the pitch-black alley before telling him what happened.

"Remember that white bitch we met at my cousin's pool party up in Pine Crest?"

"The one with the flat ass, rocking a thong?" Cream questioned, trying not to chuckle as he remembered how everyone was clowning the girl's iron board backside.

"Yeah" War promptly responded, "Yo, her ass might be flat as hell, but her pockets are swollen! I'm glad your uncle didn't cook all the powder cause she copped all that shit and you know I over charged her stinkin' ass. When she tasted it the bitch went crazy. Yo I wish I knew Jack's connect cause heads love that fish burn. We should put our money together and hop in the game, yo I'm working on this new hustle so we can get that Oprah type money *feel me*?"

"I told you I'm not fuckin' around with your nickel and dime schemes no more. Why the fuck should I pump blow if I already got a lil' money? Cream rhetorically asked.

"To get more muthafucka' what else!" War answered, "anyway she's supposed to hook me up with this other dude who she said got mad loot. I was thinkin' about just robbin' his ass instead of sellin' him shit, but as soon as he calls me it's on."

"Yeah, yeah yeah whatever. Just don't have me involved. Things were goin' good for me and now Ma'ati's pissed cause of you."

Cream stopped talking when he heard a noise over the fence. He looked to see if anyone was behind there, but it was clear. Instead of going back into the after-hours they both walked down the alley toward the front where Cream parked the car.

"Yo I almost forgot to tell you, Vera came by here looking for you earlier. She had like twenty little kids in your truck pumping Soca music like they were goin' to the West Indian day parade. I don't know why you sweatin' Ma when you got a grown woman on your dick like Vera."

"Did you tell her where I was?"

"All I said was you were out of town" War replied, as if he did say something and didn't want to fess up to it.

When they got back to the car Bing-O was leaning on Vera's coupe pouring Hennessy on the curb as a form of libation for all the people that were killed on the Avenue while he was bidding upstate. Some grimy type looking cats that knew Bing-O and Warren rolled up three trucks deep asking if they wanted to go with them to Pleasant Moments, a strip bar not too far from the Pit. Before the impetuous convoy pulled off, Warren hopped in and told Cream to beep him if anything comes up. Bing-O tried to coerce Cream into going with them, but Cream said he was done for the night and was taking it to bed.

# Scene Eleven

**After parking Vera's coupe** carefully in the dusty driveway, Cream got out and checked it for scratches and dents after those wild ass Brooklyn kids jumped all over it. He removed some footprints from the roof of the car using the same rag to wipe off the splashed mud splattered on his own rims.

Cream always kept his ride spotless. He spent a small fortune on the truck and took extra care of the twenty-six inch chrome Trump rims that it sat on. Warren was the one who convinced him that his spinner rims were old and that he should be the first one in Bridgeport to rock the new pendulous rims that swung back and forth like the mechanics of a clock whenever the vehicle came to a halt.

Using the house key that Vera awarded him after she achieved four orgasms in one night only two weeks into the relationship, Cream leisurely opened the door tiptoeing inside. It was late and Vera was sound asleep. He quietly slipped into bed without waking her. He thought. Vera was lying on her side with her back to him eyes wide open only acting like she was sleep. She rolled over once placing her arm across his chest before she really fell asleep.

In the morning Cream stood at attention like the Washington monument. Vera was up too. She nuzzled her face around his private area taking sniffs of his dick then decided to sneak him into her mouth while he lay there exposed and hard. Vera started rocking the microphone, blowing her tune so to speak as Cream tossed and turned. He was dreaming of Ma'ati and at first he couldn't tell if it was reality or not. He kept his eyes closed until he reached the climax point.

"Awwhh ahh ah!" he moaned, almost hollering Ma'ati's name by mistake.

After the inundation of sperm, Vera stood up stretching her arms behind her.

"Me jus' say good mornin'" she said with half a smile saluting Cream's falling meat soldier.

"I was gonna' wake ya', but me see ya' was up already."

She placed one of her thick chocolate legs up on the bed asking Cream if he would care for a little breakfast. With a sexy glare in her eye, Vera was hinting toward the notion of oral reciprocity.

Cream put on his boxers fronting like he didn't understand what she was implying.

"Oh I get it now Vera," Cream laughed unenthusiastically.

Vera sucked her teeth before balling up and throwing his wife beater undershirt at him in frustration.

"Too late now b'woy ya' ruin the mood if me have ta' ask."

Cream still had Ma'ati on his mind and didn't really feel like going down on Vera anyway.

"So where ya' been all day and night?" Vera inquired, "me call ya' seven times, me even swing by one ya' corna' place, but no Raheem 'n no car.

Where da' hell ya' been in me damn car?" She hollered.

"I was with a friend," he answered bluntly, suspecting Warren mentioned something to her already.

"Chauffeurin' bitches?" She retorted, "me told ya' not ta' use my tings for ya' lil' drug excursions or what have ya'!" Vera shouted flipping on him some more.

"Look baby" Cream complained, "it's too early for me to be going through this bullshit right now. Chill for a minute before you wake up the block."

She had it with him and kept on with the madness regardless. He politely removed Vera's manicured fingernail she had pressed into the side of his face.

"Will you stop with all the bitches stuff? Yes, I drove to the city, I even filled your tank with premium and I didn't get no tickets or have any drugs up in your car like you think."

"Did ya' fill that bitch with premium dick, Mr. lova'man? Ya' best not have me damn car smelling like fish cake pum' pum' ya 'ear!" Vera walked out the room.

When she stopped by the block yesterday, War accidentally let her know that Cream was with a female friend in NYC. This morning she smelled his dick for another woman's scent, but it was clean. When he moved restlessly she thought he was waking up so she played it off giving him head. It was really an act of desperation to keep Cream around, cause lately he wasn't that affectionate. She felt he was involved with someone else and all of her friends warned her that he was too young to be tied down, but Vera thought she could prove them wrong.

Her friends were right. Cream wasn't ready to have a serious relationship. Well not with her at least. If it weren't for the multi orgasmic sex he and Vera shared, there would not be a relationship at all. Vera was the type to keep it tight and she never cheated on Cream or any man she was involved with for that matter, cause she didn't want to be cheated on. She'd rather break off the relationship than have to creep. Cream didn't cheat per se, but lately he'd been stepping out looking for something else. He leaned against the kitchen counter rubbing the back of his neck.

"Vera I'm not lying to you I was with a friend yesterday. We were visiting her family and stuff like that."

"Nuff!" she yelled, "I had it!"

In the beginning of their relationship Vera thought that she might be able to mold Cream into the man that her children's father wasn't, but she was wrong. It was a wrap. Cream never turned down a sexual episode with her plus his shirt smelled like the cocoa mango oil Ma'ati was wearing, she suspected he was with another woman no matter what he came up with.

Pacing back and forth, Vera revealed that the only reason she started looking for Cream yesterday was because she left some signed permission slips in the glove compartment. She had that island fire in her eyes and would cut you in a minute. Out of the many things that Cream didn't know about her was that she had stabbed the shit out of her ex husband twice, sending him to the hospital when he messed around on her.

Vera grabbed a letter opener that was sitting on the kitchen table gripping it tight in her fist. She moved toward Cream who had his back to her peeling an orange over the trashcan.

"Vera I have something to tell you...I met someone the other day."

Cream was hesitant at first then turned to look Vera in the face only seconds before she was to stab him in his back. She dropped the sharp letter opener creating a metal sound on the cold kitchen floor. Cream looked down at the silver letter opener in shock. He could not believe that she was going to actually cut him.

Vera started crying as she fell into his grasp. Cream held her tightly letting her release. The scorned woman was sick and tired of frivolous relationships and it showed. Most men Cream's age and beyond would kill to be with a beautiful woman such as Vera. She had it together and all, but it wasn't that. Even though Cream had just met Ma'ati, her alluring energy captured his heart. Vera captured his dick. The mental stimulation beat the temporary physical pleasure this time. The key is balance. Ma'ati stimulated Cream's mind and now he was curious if she could put it down between the sheets, *balance*.

He held Vera's head tightly against his chest the harder she cried. At that moment he realized that in order to truly respect a women like that, he had to leave her alone so she could grow with a man who was willing to love her and give her the respect that she really deserved. The black woman he was ready to give his everything to probably thought he was some foul street nigga who used women then threw them away he thought. After releasing tears of reprieve Vera stated that it was time to end the games. She didn't have to say it was over cause they both knew it. There was relief in her voice and Cream was lucky that he told her the truth before she jigged his ass in the back.

"I respect everything that you said and I know what this means," Cream reposed.

He handed her the key that she gave him then went into the bedroom to pack his stuff.

While packing clothes together they both laughed about what her friends were going to say when they found out about the highly anticipated break up. Cream was happy to know Vera wasn't going to hold a grudge against him. She wasn't heart broken at all she said that she'd been through that already. She just hated to be lied to.

Rather than drag out another unhealthy relationship Vera only wanted Cream to be truthful with her from the beginning. To Cream's benefit being with Vera added maturity to his stature and for the first time in his life he wanted to be with a woman whom he wanted nothing from except her time. He kissed Vera on the cheek exchanging one last tight hug before heading out the door.

# Scene Twelve

**Weeks passed since** Cream and Vera parted ways. Warren had been trying to contact his PNC, being that the last time he had seen him was that night at the Pit. Cream was out of town and had been laying low, not bothering with anyone. He had booked a room and stayed at the Foxwoods Casino for two weeks. Before coming home he took a trip to the Niantic Correctional Center to visit his favorite woman. Cream's mother had been down for about thirteen months with eleven more to go. After a news exposé blew up welfare fraud in Connecticut, mad people started to get hit for beating the system and his moms happened to be one of them.

Cream hated visiting anyone in prison, let alone his own mother. Being that Drusilla was a level 2, the visiting arrangements were unrestrained with no glass between them or a phone to talk through. Dressed in brown prison garb with the bold letters NCC stamped on the front, Drusilla gave her son a big hug and kiss as soon as she entered the room.

"Raheem! I'm so glad you came. Let me look at you," she said taking a step back.

It had only been two months since the last time Drusilla seen her son, but she was excited as if it had been years. Prison will do that to a person after being around the same people everyday, talking about the same things day in and day out.

The correction officer let them know immediately that they were hugging too long then ushered them to sit down.

"I can't stand punk ass C.O's. On the brick they act like bitches, oh I'm sorry mom pardon my language, I just can't stand them faggots. "

"For a lack of better words you're right. You should see how they set up fights in here. Let me tell you, the female guards are worst than the men!" Drusilla expounded.

Under the table which they sat, Drusilla slipped off the old shower shoes she wore, exchanging them with Cream for a pair of brand new sneakers he had forced his feet into. His heel was sticking all the way out the back and the guard never noticed how silly he looked walking through the door.

The Department of Corrections had stopped allowing inmates to receive footwear of any type from the outside. They wanted to make money for themselves forcing inmates to purchase Big M state sneakers and shower shoes through the commissary.

"Do you know how hard it is to squeeze my size 12 foot into a women's size 8?" Cream frowned.

"So how is everybody?" Drusilla had to laugh at the face her son made describing the ordeal.

"They're good. How 'bout you ma?" Cream replied.

"Well I finally got a job. It took me ten months to get outside clearance, but I got it. I'm working at this restaurant called Café 24 and would you believe it's inside the D.O.C headquarters? They got us cooking for these bastards, but I don't mind though, cause I'm eating lovely myself. I had me a stuffed omelet this morning for breakfast and fish & chips for lunch. Shoot, I can drink as much bottled water and juice that I want."

"That sounds nice, I know it beats sitting around the dayroom watching stupid soap operas and stuff" Cream commented.

Drusilla seemed to be doing the time and not letting the time do her. She used her temporary confinement to get her head together and decide what she was going to do once released. She told her son that she was writing a book and would one day like to have it published. Unlike some of the other women that let themselves go in prison, Drusilla kept it together. Cream and his mother shared the same glowing brown complexion and there was no way anyone could say that they didn't look alike.

"Well tell me baby, are you involved yet?" Drusilla asked her son, "don't have me waiting 'till I'm ninety, then tell me I'm going to be a grandma Raheem."

Cream started twisting his mustache hair and whenever he did that his mother knew that he wanted to talk about something.

"What's wrong baby, I'm your mother and you know I know when you're keeping something from me?"

"Its this girl, I mean I'm really feelin' her and everything, but I don't know. I don't think she sees it like that. We had a misunderstanding and its probably going to be impossible to get her to see how I truly feel about things," Cream explained.

A fat blonde picking her nose was staring at

them, all in their conversation like she knew Cream. Drusilla gave the nosy dyke a project look ready to curse the bitch out.

"Mind your own damn business! Don't make me act a fool up in here you nasty slob!"

Drusilla turned her attention back to Cream with a smile.

"Don't worry about it baby, the impossible just takes a little longer, you'll see. If you're meant to be together you'll eventually be together."

They talked about family and other things as the visit flew by.

"*Visiting hours will be over in five minutes*," a voice was heard over the loud speaker.

Drusilla hugged her son goodbye for the remainder of the visit.

"I love you mom, I'll see you in three weeks. Don't get caught spitting in the food," Cream laughed.

"Other girls in here do more than spit in the food, they should be grateful that I'm not disgusting like that."

A butch looking guard escorted the women away as they all waved bye to their families up until the last second. For the entire drive back, Cream thought about his life and how unhappy he'd been feeling lately. When he got back to Bridgeport he finally checked his messages and decided to call Warren back.

"Where you at kid?" Warren answered the phone.

"Behind you," Cream acknowledged.

War looked in the rear view seeing that Cream was pulling up behind him. He frowned at the out of character three-piece suit and tie Warren was wearing.

"Damn, a little coke and some paper got niggas dressing like the godfather and shit. What's up with the suit, you look like you're ready for a funeral" Cream voiced.

"Act like you know nigga!" War retorted, "Ajax wake is at five o'clock."

It had slipped Cream's mind that his friend's wake was today. Ajax was a mutual friend that hung out with them from time to time. Back in the day they used to all play tackle football on cement and steal bikes together. Ajax had been shot in the back by a racist New Haven police officer several days ago. Even so, Cream had promised himself that he would stop attending funerals and wakes six friends ago, but knew he had to hit Jax's wake.

"Of course I'm goin' pick me up from my aunt's crib in like half an hour. I'ma take a shower and get dressed."

He headed home, while War stayed parked in front of his house drinking from a bottle of Henessey Paradis extra attempting to drink away the anger and pain. Earlier in the day the police commissioner had one of his crooked goon lieutenants shake down the Ave, forcing Warren to cough up a couple of thousand.

Since Vera's place was unavailable for facilitating, Cream was back at his aunt and uncle's spot temporally. As he started staying out all night gambling, eventually not coming home at all, his aunt told him that it was either in or out. She said that her place was nobody's flophouse. Cream had enough money saved to move out a long time ago and only planned on staying there until he decided what he was going to do.

"Get your leg off the side of the couch!" Cream yelled at one of Ray's friends like he was

Aunt Simone busting up their little party, "What are all these beer cans doing on my coffee table?" He continued.

Uncle Ray was in the living room watching TV with a few of his drinking buddies. The first thing out of Ray's mouth was, "Some white boy came by here asking for you a few hours ago...now look boy, I don't get in your business, but you better not be having no transaction bullshit anywhere around this house! You got that Cream?"

He thought Ray was fooling around until he seen how serious his face was.

"Never let a fiend know where you rest your head" Unk scolded, "especially when it ain't even your goddamn house!"

"You know I would never do anything that stupid," Cream riposted. He thought it was really strange because no one ever came by the house looking for him except Warren.

Ray's friends were into TV. They could care less who came by or who was selling what out of where. Simone walked into the room using a dishtowel to wipe flour from her arms and wrists.

"Lenny...get your damn foot off my table!" she hollered, "You need to put that drink down and watch TV in your own living room."

Simone had a country accent even though she wasn't from the south. Her mother moved up north from *South Cack-a-lacka'* back in the day and it rubbed off on her.

"Get over here and give your auntie some suga boy!" She pushed Cream into the kitchen, stirring up her greens again while she talked with her nephew.

"How's my sister doin'? Did you tell her I couldn't make it cause I went to check on mama?"

"No auntie I didn't. I didn't want her to be worrying about grandma in there. You know how she gets, but mom's is doin' ai'ight. She got a lil' job now and everything, but how was the flight?"

"Good. God is good. I was able to bring a surprise back with me too."

Simone had just returned home from an emergency trip down south yesterday. Cream's grandmother's sugar was high and they had to rush her to the hospital, so Simone went down to make sure everything was okay.

"Excuse me auntie I'm in a rush, I'll eat later. I gotta' take a shower and get dressed real fast okay."

Cream sped up the stairs. He took a quick hot shower then donned the only suit that he had, which was his black double-breasted Armani suit. It was two years old, but still looked crisp. Everybody in his family called it "the funeral suit" cause they knew what time it was when he wore it.

While Cream incessantly searched his dresser drawer for a pair of nice dress socks, War was outside blowing the horn like a mad man. He rushed down the stairs through the kitchen like a bat outta' hell. Simone noticed Cream in his suit and gave the mashed potatoes a break.

"Don't tell me another one of your hard headed friends was murdered again?" She put both hands on her hips and huffed, "Raheem you hear me talking to you? *What that boy needs is a nice young lady to keep him out the darn street all day and night before he gets his behind locked away or worse*" Simone thought, "you be careful now ya' heard me?"

Cream gave his aunt a fast kiss and bounced as if he heard her say that a million times before.

*********

Meanwhile, Bridgeport's political scene was experiencing technical difficulties. The streets were organizing from the inside out. *The inside of prison that is*. Over the years that crack impregnated the hoods with misery and champagne wishes simultaneously, millions of black men got swept into the prison system between the two sentiments. Many brothers that got knocked did revolving bids, which meant they would do a year come home and do the same shit again. Prison became a second home for some and a coffin for others. Although some heads unplugged from the tier blocks and mess halls using their time to gain a knowledge of self, others swirled into families and crews were created.

The system would call these types of families gangs if you let them tell it and by the time the crack game was at its zenith in Bridgeport, three major so-called gangs had spilled out onto the city streets. A couple of families were statewide and even national like the Latin Kings and Brotherhood. Jamaican posses like the Cats and Rats made noise, but smaller crews like the Body Snatchers, Bush Mob, Madd Brothers, Foundation and Pump Nation kept shit raw in Bridgeport. They went all out for whatever, but sadly enough the wrong people got hurt.

It took a lot of jail time and many deaths, but heads had finally realized that unity amongst them was the key to so-called "making it." But when they tried forming a unified organization, the union loosened just as fast because members were turning up dead everyday. Someone was assassinating heads all over town. The papers reported that most of the bodies found were bound and gagged executed military style.

# Scene Thirteen

**Cream slammed the door** hard by accident when he got into Warren's Nissan Maxima.

"Damn! Break my doors off next time!"

Cream smiled turning the music back up, as War passed him what was left of the expensive cognac. At this time Warren was feeling pretty good speaking his mind.

"I'm tired of these fuckin' police killing my niggas and robbing us every night! If those bastards run up on me again...word is bond son, I'm bustin' back."

Cream wiped his mouth after gulping down the rest of the Henny.

"I hear you son. The shit is getting ridiculous. They're clappin' heads like its going out of style, but I never knew they ran up on you the first time?"

War never responded and pulled into the back of the mortuary where they ended up parking. Enjoying a nice buzz, Cream continued his hood evaluation delving into more personal matters.

"I was thinking about the future yo and I think..."

Before Cream could conclude what he was

going to say, War rudely interrupted.

"The future is all about gettin' paid you know what I mean? Once I shine I wanna' keep it that way," Warren uttered with a minor slur.

"Everything that glitters ain't gold my neezy. Money ain't shit if you don't know what to do with it...do you think the police be robbing niggas just for money? Everything they do is about control," Cream stated belligerently.

Warren lit a cigarette then let Cream finish what he wanted to say this time.

"How much doe you got stashed right now?" Cream asked.

"I don't know," War calculated, "I'll say about nine thousand plus the product thats left? I'll say about eighteen."

"Damn that's it! What happened to all that fuckin' money I helped you count six months ago? That was like forty five thousand right there?"

Cream was stunned in a suspicious way after Warren just shrugged his shoulders like he didn't know what happened to all his money.

"The last time I counted I had a little under eighty, but the reason that I asked was cause I wanted to make you a proposition."

"Thousand!" War dubiously inquired, "you telling me you got *eighty thousand* in your aunt's crib right now?"

Cream was vigilant in his response this time, since Warren seemed to act funny when asked about his own stack.

"Who said anything about my aunt's house? All I said was I got eighty gee's put up somewhere. See I know how to save my money kid. I don't waste my shit on jewelry and cheap overpriced gear like you be doin'. I'm tryna' start a business and step up my game!"

"What type of business?" Warren asked, "pharmaceuticals...what nigga talk to me baby."

"If you let me talk I'll tell you! The drug game shit is over yo face it, how many times did we see big time niggas around here get popped over dumb shit cause they stayed stuck on stupid. You ain't stuntin' just cause you buy mad shit...if a nigga never built anything or established anything that lasted in the hood longer than they did, how gangsta' is that?"

Warren smirked like he wasn't feeling what his partner was getting at.

"Our money don't mean shit no matter how much we got if we don't use it right. It's only a tool. Watch the signals when the color of money changes. The government could just tell us our money is no good...or they could just take our shit and lie about it. Whenever they wanna' get you, even though they don't have shit on you, they go create false evidence anyway. Take the Jones boys for example or look at Frankie and them. The paper reported that they found ten mill cash in his crib and more in his club. You don't think the FEDS took some money off the top? Learn the golden rule son *he who has the gold makes the rules.*"

War waved his hand to bypass everything Cream had said.

"Yo you ain't been acting right ever since you met that Ma'ati chick. I knew you all my life Cream and I never heard you talk like this before. I think that girl put some shit in your head. I see she kept the money I gave her from Tootsie's crib though," Warren chuckled, "she knows what time it is like everybody else...the dollar is mutha'fuckin' boss all over the world! Why shouldn't I chase it?" War dissented, "I'm not tryna' be a poor lint ball nigga all my life."

Cream just shook his head disdainfully. He knew Warren wasn't dirt poor and that he went through more money than people's fathers made in a year working a decent job. War didn't seem to understand Cream at this point and him being bent did not help out either. Without Cream's vigilance, Warren would have evaporated all of his funds on gear, hotels, jewelry or anything else that he thought accentuated his gaudy image.

"Ma'ati had nothin' to do with it," Cream lashed back, "you think I'm tryna' end up like Russell and Adrian!" He exclaimed.

Russell Peeler and his brother Adrian Peeler grew up on the North End close to Warren's crib. As the sons of a respectable female police officer, the Peelers were basically good dudes back then. The game made them financially rich quick and spiritually poor just as fast. Russell was convicted for shooting an acquaintance dead, as he sat in a barber's chair getting a haircut.

The victim's 8 year-old son was to testify against Russell after witnessing a prior attempt on his father's life and that's when the inconceivable occurred. Russell supposedly put the hit out on the little boy. His brother Adrian escaped from a halfway house in Hartford, CT and supposedly executed both the boy and his mother. The case received national attention and caused Cream to really think about things. If he didn't slow down and invest time and money into his future foundation, there wouldn't be one for him to stand on.

"Not for nothin' yo, but the dollar is not boss all over the world!" Cream emphasized, as he dropped it on War technically for ridiculing his statement.

"What YOU call the almighty dollar is in fact a Federal Reserve Note. In actuality it has no real value at all, because it's only a promissory note, a fuckin' piece of paper promising to pay whatever amount it is that you spend and by the way the Federal Reserve is not *federal* at all. It's a privately owned banking system" Cream laughed, "you thought the dollar was backed by gold and silver? The money we got in our pocket right now was designed by the Federal Reserve to create debt through inflation. Every time we spend money we're legally promising to pay that amount, like writing a check against a closed account. What happens is, you and the rest of the citizens of the nation end up owing. Its uncommonly known as the National Debt, check it out. Basicly what it does is transfer power and control to a small elite group of old men that run the entire world's power structure and economy. Why do you think they call money currency son? Just like electrical current, currency makes shit operate and do whatever they want niggas to do."

The saying *as long as I owe you you'll never go broke* is the truth. As long as you're in debt, the people you owe will always have power over you. Warren didn't give a fuck and was tired of hearing what sounded like gibberish to him. He turned his attention to the people going into the funeral home.

"That makes no sense at all. Who told you that bullshit...Ma'ati?" He asked.

"Actually it was an accountant that schooled me," Cream articulated, "the pretty executive who worked for Fleet Bank. You remember the one I was slayin' last year, the thick honey with the Rover? I'm just saying we should make the money work for us instead of working for the money that's all."

It was obvious to Cream that Warren could care less about his future. War was a 'now' person. He seemed content dabbling in petty drug sales and swindling women all his life. He wasn't trying to hear anything, especially anything about money being created to control a person physically and mentally. It's hard to convince blind minds that money is only an illusion of power. Its what you do with it that makes you powerful.

# Scene Fourteen

**People sat inside the funeral** home for hours listening to community sellouts speak the bullshit, while others mourned the loss of their family member and comrade. Even War had tears in his eyes thinking about his older brother who was also shot and killed by police in the P.T Barnum housing projects when he was 11. The entire service was crowded with black people from all over the area. It was a sad event of course, but most attendees were more angry than sad. This was the area's third shooting this month of an unarmed black man killed by police.

Reverend Budsac spoke to the mourners about how most police officers were actually good guys and that it was a sin to have animosity toward the officers who shot these young men. Ajax's father stood up in awe of the Rev's outrageous eulogy. This was the same Reverend Budsac that sniffed on the low and was known to have "relations" with many of the ladies in his congregation. Nobody was trying to hear the crap the Rev was putting down, so the crowd started to get loud in objection.

Cream and Warren paid their respects. They viewed the body then consoled Ajax's parents as they passed by the front row. Ajax's mother was more than vexed that her son lay dead in a casket because some hotheaded trigger-happy rookie decided to fly off the handle. She had blood in her eye like *George Jackson*, shaking in her seat boiling with anger. The more the Reverend spoke, the more people began walking out to take their dissatisfaction elsewhere.

Besides those that worked with the crooked police department, people of all nationalities living in the area couldn't stand cops because they seemed to always start shit. The largest part of the police force that patrolled the streets didn't even live in Bridgeport. They were mostly from the suburbs and viewed black people from how they're portrayed on the big screen or television.

Tension was brewing outside. Between all the dirty shootings and political corruption the local media had recently exposed, tempers were on the verge of explosion. Two officers with a K-9 riding shotgun drove by the service slowly and one of the asshole cops motioned with his hand like it was a gun, pointing his finger out of the window as the dog barked unremittingly.

"Yo did you see that muthafucka' try to mark us!" a person in the crowd hollered.

Seconds later the wake turned to furor after shots were fired at the cops by one of Ajax's grieving friends. The police shot back into the air and people scattered all over the place, some running out of the funeral parlor before they even got to pay their respects.

Warren moved out of the way as a group of young kids ran passed him down the block. He stood out front of Pettway's Variety to warn Bing-O that the Police were on their way down the block. Bing-O was talking to Geek on a payphone about somebody he was planning to victimize.

Cream watched the commotion from inside the car waiting for War to return from the store. Being that vehicles had them blocked in he couldn't move the car until everyone else pulled out. Warren strolled back to the car smoking a loose cig with a bottle of beer in his hand.

"Who was shootin' yo?" he asked nonchalantly.

"I don't know" Cream replied, "whoever it was dipped down Baldwin."

They weren't going anywhere no time soon cause the police were shaking down mourners as they exited the service and the parking lot was still packed. A rusted Toyota Corolla parked next to them had a 14-year-old in the back seat with his head tilted back, looking up at the drooping upholstery. All Cream saw was a woman's head bopping up and down.

"Oh shit, that looks like Miss Tucker," he uttered after recognizing the woman in the car.

Warren straightened up in his seat to see what Cream was talking about. The young trick handed the woman two loose fraggles (crack rocks) before she got out, spitting semen on the ground.

"Damn when she start cluckin'?" War stated, as if he was missing out on something good.

Cream acted like he didn't notice Miss Tucker when she looked at him by turning his head the other way.

"*Tap Tap Tap*!" Miss Tucker banged on the window glass.

"Hey baby, how we doing today" she asked, "you boys want yo ding dongs sucked? I'll do ya' nice and good. Roll down the window so I can talk to you for a minute baby."

Cream let the window down backing away as Miss Tucker tried to kiss him on the cheek.

"What do you want Miss T, does June know you're out hear actin' like this?" Cream said, blowing up her spot.

Miss Tucker widened her eyes when he mentioned her son's name. She was high as a kite and up until now, she hadn't recognized her former fifth grade student.

"Uuh, I wanted to ask you if I can borrow ten dollars," she asked while scratching her chest and the side of her neck, "cause um, they're gettin' ready to turn my lights off and um, I need to see if I'm gonna' correct homework papers."

Cream knew she wanted to buy more drugs, so he dissed her ass. Before Miss T left she asked them again if they were sure that they didn't want to have a good time with her. After getting the message that nothing was happening, she walked away tapping on another car window to pull the same stunt.

"Damn, what the fuck happened to us? That lady used to be one of my favorite teachers in grade school," Cream revealed.

"Crack happened nigga!" Warren cheered, "that's why I only sell drugs to white people now, cause that shit got muthafucka's around here buggin' the fuck out! Plus they be broke. Yo I heard some base head stabbed Biffy over one slab yesterday."

"I'm telling you son, we don't need that energy in our circle. And don't sleep either...white people steal entire continents. What makes you think they won't kill your ass over a couple of grams?"

Cream was determined to convince his a-alike, that he should leave the street grind behind him. He wanted to use the money he already accumulated doing dirt for something more virtuous. Warren played along with Cream hoping to skip another one of his boys exhausting lectures.

"Maybe we can set up a basketball clinic for the young dudes who love to ball," Warren thought out loud playing the role.

Cream's thoughts were far from that. He was thinking on another level.

"Please!" Cream reacted insulted, "how many niggas they got in the NBA right now?"

"A lot," War estimated.

"Then tell me why do so many NBA cats set up basketball centers in the hood, when they know it's one out of a million that actually make it to the NBA? Wouldn't it make more sense to establish something more people could succeed in? How in the hell can you come off with one in a million odds!" Cream articulated.

He wasn't far from the truth. Most athletes and entertainers that came from the hood rarely built a foundation that had an overwhelming impact on the lives of black people.

"I don't care what kind of job you got, if you sign a contract you're agreeing not to bite the hand that feeds you. Peep how all the athletes and actors that made power moves, got shut off like light switches soon after."

"You might be right on this one" Warren addressed, "look what happened to Jordan when he dissed Nike and tried to retire. His pops mysteriously got kilt...c'mon a car jacking in the middle of the fuckin' desert!"

"Bill Cosby's son was supposedly jacked too don't forget," Cream recapped, "when he tried to buy 'The Little Rascals' and NBC. Something mysterious like that even happened to Dr. J's son?"

It was time to bounce. Conspiracy theory time was over. The jam-packed parking lot emptied and they were finally able to pull off after sitting there for forty minutes.

"About time!" Cream yawned, "My ass was starting to stick to the seat. Does the AC ever work in this bucket?"

Warren paid Cream's jokes no mind and kept rolling down the window. He didn't care what anybody thought about his car cause he had a different one every other month. The Maxima that he drove was a chop shop special that only ran him $1000. In high school War had hooked up with this oily Arab mechanic that traded luxurious stolen cars teens brought him, for somewhat legal shoddy style rides, which were basically vehicles made out of stolen car parts with phony paperwork.

The Avenue was getting flooded. Everybody from Ajax's wake started to hang out on the sidewalks. It looked like a Freaknik meets Bike Week had taken over the Ave. Girls were everywhere and players were stopping their cars to rap to every chick out there.

"You see that chick in front of the Jackson club?" War pointed.

"Who the one with the mean stance talking to Dirty Roy?" Cream confirmed.

"Yeah. I keep seeing her everywhere I go," Warren sounded perplexed, "the first time was in Tipton's a couple of months ago and then she started poppin' up all over like she's following me?"

"Whoever she is, somebody's hitting her pockets off with all types of loot or she hit the lottery? Would you take a look at that fuckin' Benz!"

The mysterious woman they were referring to was Kali, a new chick on the scene that had that "rich bitch I'm the wife of a don" look. Mad cars and trucks were pulling over and beeping at Kali making an effort to get with her, but she dissed them only giving the top drug dealers the time of day. Warren continued to drive slowly the entire time he was talking. He paid no attention to the cars that were honking behind him to speed up.

When he circled the block, he slowed down even more just to get a better glimpse of Kali who was leaning on her pink SL 55 AMG Mercedes Benz. It was fully hooked of course with 22-inch Benetto rims gleaming, TV and navigation system in the steering wheel and all that. Kali winked as Warren drove by staring at her ride.

Cream requested that War stop by his house before they went anywhere else so he could change his clothes and strap up, given that so many strange faces were in the area. War was talking to someone on his cell and momentarily said to Cream that he would park around the corner, since there were some youngsters riding dirt bikes up and down the street doing wheelies and tricks. It was only a hop skip and a jump for Cream to walk to his spot anyway, so it wasn't a problem.

Cream crunched glass as he walked confidently in his dress shoes stepping through the narrow path that led to his aunt's house. The dogs barking were nerve racking, but there was something more threatening and odd. Geek was standing on the back steps of Cream's aunt's house peeking into the kitchen window. The demented looking white boy turned toward him with a .22 in his grip after hearing Cream accidentally kick a tin can. Cream knew what time it was now, but what he didn't know was how he was going to escape without getting shot. Before he could turn around to jet, Geek let off two shots in his direction.

"Get your ass over here! Where you think you going nigga?" Geek yelled, firing another shot.

Panicking because his gun was still in the house, Cream cut ass back down the narrow pathway. The whole time he just knew he was definitely going to get it in the back. Keenly reacting he lunged through a piece of dry-rot plywood that barricaded the entrance to an abandoned garage. The fiends inside the garage dropped the needle they were sharing, looking just as nervous as Cream was as he crashed to the floor creating a large dust cloud.

Seconds before Cream dove inside, Geek fired two more shots, which ricocheted off the outside of the garage. No sooner than Geek could get off another shot, a loud ear popping blast went off.

"BLLOOOOMMM!" Echoed the sound down the path like thunder.

"AARRHH MY GOD! My leg! Ahhhh! My fucking leg!" Geek yelled intensely.

Uncle Raymond had let loose his 12-gauge Mossberg from the top balcony. It overlooked the backyard and pathway, which gave him a clear shot. In excruciating pain, the cornball assassin limped away on one leg. He hopped past the garage where Cream lay on the ground unnoticed with a 2X4 in his grip ready to swing. When Warren heard the shots he rose up as if he was sober. He grabbed his loaded 9mm from under the seat at the same time that Cream ran out into the street pointing and yelling. For a brief moment he had his gun pointed at Cream then lowered it.

"Get that nigga Yo! He tried to take me out" hollered Cream, as Geek hopped toward the get away car.

In a flash Warren floored the gas crushing Geek between his car and theirs. Like a trained hit man he then let off his entire clip into the passenger side window and Geek's body at the same time. The driver had one hand on the wheel, hanging half out the car with all types of fluids gushing from the side of his head. The entire ordeal seemed to last an eternity, but actually went down in less than a minute.

After the first shots were fired no one was in sight to witness Warren and Cream speed off down the block. Whenever there was a shoot out in the hood, people of all ages knew the drill, stop and drop. Another rule of wisdom was you didn't see shit...even if you witnessed everything.

# Scene Fifteen

"**You, hit yo?"**

"Nah I'm straight," Cream answered War out of breath.

He advised him to slow down so they didn't look so obvious fleeing the scene. Warren cruised passed Newfield Park like nothing even happened.

"I don't know what made that kid think he could come to the East End with a little ass twenty two. What the fuck was he thinking?" War stated hyped up.

"I should have known something was up when Unk told me some white boy came by the house lookin' for me," Cream exclaimed.

There were spent gun shells all over the car. Some stuck between the seats, a few in the utility tray and even some on the dash.

"Let's get rid of the heat right now, drive by the bridge and I'll toss it," Cream suggested.

"Fuck it I don't care, that shit got bodies on it anyway. What I want to know is who let off that cannon?" Warren wondered.

"I'm pretty sure that was Unk," Cream affirmed, "His pump is loud as hell. When I heard that shit I thought somebody blew up a quarter stick of dynamite!"

"Yo, Uncle Ray is 'bout it 'bout it," War

laughed.

As they rolled over the bridge, Cream tossed a handful of shells and War's 9mm into the Yellow Mill channel. The adrenaline rush was still pulsating. Cream was engrossed in the thought of almost losing his life, while Warren drove down East Main St. War offered Cream a cigarette to calm his nerves, but he declined.

"I gotta' get out this damn suit" Cream complained, "I almost bust my ass sliding in these slippery ass shoes."

He showed Warren the bullet hole in his sleeve, grateful that it was the suit that had the hole in it and not him. After stripping down to his undershirt Cream decided to head downtown for some new gear. Warren agreed to patronize Halls sportswear, a black father & son business, only reason being was that Cream said he would treat. Cream always made the effort to support black business whenever possible, instead of handing his money over to others so easily.

Warren on the other hand thought that a white person's ice cubes were colder than a black person's ice cubes and would happily dump piles of cash into their registers just for the sake of being white. Of course if you're a white retailer that automatically makes your merchandise "official" Warren thought.

When they got downtown it was flooded with people shopping like it was the first of the month. After paying for both of the throwback jerseys as well as both pair of jeans and fresh pairs of city's, they left their suits in a dumpster outside of the Arcade mall.

Before they got in the car Warren spotted another glimmering pink Mercedes. This one was a

G500 SUV with New York plates too but had Ma'ati getting into it.

"Yo ain't that shorty over there son?" Warren uttered, while lacing up his new feet.

"Let's try catching them at the light."

War pulled up behind the G5 at the stoplight. He beeped the horn three times as the truck pulled off. Four blocks later and tired of beeping, he decided to pull along side of them in the on-coming traffic lane. The chinky eyed sista' pushing the Benz hollered out the window like Warren was an idiot.

"Take a picture next time asshole!" she screamed, "It'll last longer muthafucka'!" Then she sped off.

Ma'ati recognized Cream waving his arm out the window and asked her sister to pull over. Michelle pulled to the curb and Cream carelessly crossed the street walking over to the passenger side.

"Raheem are you crazy?" Ma asked.

"Yeah what's up with your friend driving like he don't got no sense! He almost caused an accident driving on the opposite side of the road," Shell snapped.

"Could you please follow us, we have to talk about some real shit," Cream claimed.

Ma'ati smelled liquor on Cream's breath causing her to frown. By the look in his eye she could tell that he was serious. With uncertainty Shell agreed to follow. Warren led them all the way down Fairfield Avenue crossing the city limits into a cheesy motel parking lot. Michelle complained somewhat, sucking her teeth like she wasn't feeling the situation.

"Got me up in some motel parking lot. I just

know these niggas don't think they're gettin' some coochie?

"Shell that's all you think about" Ma rebuked, "Raheem jus' wanna' talk, that's all. I haven't seen him in awhile and I wanna' hear what he has to say."

Cream was in the motel office talking to the sleazy manager for a couple of minutes then came out waving everyone into a first floor room. When Warren stepped out of his car, Michelle liked what she saw and changed her disruptive tune.

"Now that's what's really good," she muttered.

Warren had a squint in his eye, thinking the same thing as he watched Michelle stride gallantly toward them. He bit down on his lip wondering how many licks it would take to get to the center of that?

Michelle's look was primetime, replicating that of her sister's striking beauty.

"Would you relax nigga," Cream mumbled, "at least wait until she gets into the room before you start droolin'."

Ma'ati, Michelle and their cousin were on their way back to Manhattan for the weekend. Ma'ati reassured her younger cousin Twana not to worry about any funny business, because she had *Prometheus*, her .380 pistol and her razor on her person. It was Friday and all three females looked vibrant, scowling as they entered the musty motel room.

"Welcome to Chump Plaza ladies...do not make yourself at home," Warren announced as the girl's walked in.

Shell was the only one who laughed at his corny jokes. Cream instructed the trio to make themselves comfortable for the time being. Warren inhaled a deep breath as he got a closer look at Michelle's mouth-watering cleavage.

"*Those things can't be real*" he thought, making eye contact with Shell who now had her legs crossed sitting on the edge of the bed. Twana, the youngest one of the three, lit a cigarette talking like she was grown.

"Cut you short nothing! Why y'all got us up in this raggedy ass motel room," she loudly voiced.

Cream didn't know where to begin. He gave Ma'ati a tight hug expressing how happy he was to see her and conveyed how much he was sorry about the misunderstanding they had the night she slammed the door in his face.

"I think you could be in danger," Cream warned, "one of Jack's flunkies tried to get at me today and I just thought you should know."

Like always, Warren cut in the conversation before Cream could finish.

"They were waitin' for my nigga" War disclosed, "they might try to see you too nah'mean?"

Cream sat down next to Ma on the bed bypassing his blabbermouth friend.

"It might not be safe staying in your building right now. I know you're a tough woman and all, but I don't think you should be alone with Jack's crew on the loose. If you let me, I'll protect all of you Ma...from head to toe."

Ma'ati smiled at her sister on the low. Shell and Twana started raising their voices in concern after Warren kept talking.

"What did you get her into? who is trying to kill you Tiara? Wait 'till daddy finds out!"

War looked at Cream then Cream looked at

War, "Daddy? That's your sister?" They asked in unison.

"Yeah that's my nosy ass sista' Michelle and this is my lil' gully ass cousin Twana."

"I'll be that, but I ain't little," Twana squeaked, "I'm sixteen you betta' recognize," she said palming her breasts.

Although one would think Twana was in her twenties from the way she dressed, her true age showed from the way that she acted. Ma'ati got up and sat down between her sister and Warren. She noticed how much Shell was sweating Warren's sex appeal and whispered in her sister's ear.

"You two should get along really well cause you love salad and he loves tossin' it."

Michelle nervously squirmed from the delightful thought. She sat wondering which way Warren licked, *"Side to side, clockwise or counter clockwise?"*

Shell had to start asking questions to change the subject, re-crossing her legs to extinguish her sudden burst of horniness.

"So tell me Warren, somebody tried to kill you?"

"Yo you should've seen it" Cream cut in this time, "after my uncle just about blew the niggas leg off, War did a Swartz-a-nigger shootin' shit up like a ghetto Terminator!"

Cream laid it on thick and it was obvious to everyone in the room that he was trying to hype up the story. After hearing the exaggerated version, Michelle asked Warren about the real story. While the two started talking amongst themselves, Ma'ati pulled Cream into the small bathroom so they could have more privacy.

"See man, that's why I got so mad at you

that night. You could get me killed doing dumb shit like that. I still don't really know what you and Action Wackson were tryin' to pull off, but that's one of the reasons why I moved out of Brooklyn. I had to get away from the bullshit niggas pull."

Cream moved her close to him trying to explain everything.

"You could ask War, I didn't even know those niggas. I never saw those kids before in my life. I'm not gonna' act like I'm a drug dealer when I'm not. Look sweetness, I just wanted to tell you that you could be in danger. I don't want anything to happen to you, cause I really like you nah'mean? You don't even know how much you've altered my consciousness already. Something activated inside of me that I can't explain. Just give me a chance."

"I have no time to play games" Ma'ati clarified, "but what you need to do is stop thinkin' about us and call your uncle to see what the deal is at home. I'm happy you're okay and I must admit that maybe I over reacted that night...I'm feeling you too and usually when that's the case, the man turns out to be an asshole."

Ma'ati kissed him on the cheek then went back into the room with everybody else. Cream thought calling the house was a good idea, so he stayed in the bathroom dialing his cell.

"Sup Whodie?"

It took Cream a moment to recognize the voice, since he hadn't seen or heard from his southern cousin Tymel in years.

"Who is this?" he asked.

"Yo cuzin Tymel, nuck'ah."

"T-Y! What's the deal...when you break north?"

"I flew up with moms yesterday. She wanted

to surprise you, but hold on cuz, pops wants to speak with you."

Uncle Ray got on the phone.

"What in the hell took you so long to call? I didn't know if you were hit or what. You okay boy? I just watched the live local news and they said those two had it coming anyway. I doubt if the police push a strong investigation cause those fools were wanted for murder and armed robbery they're damn selves. They strangled some old lady last night robbing a bodega" Ray said, "their mug shots were just on the news a minute ago. You ever heard of Omar Watkins and Earl Simsbury?"

Cream didn't know Geek's government name was Earl Simsbury, but he knew the driver Omar Watkins.

"Yeah I know his ass" Cream was sad to say.

"When I seen that ugly face staring through my window I almost had a shit hemorrhage. I was so pissed I wanted to chase him with the butter knife I was using on my toast."

Ray did most of the talking while Cream listened. After he finished telling old war stories Cream asked Unk if he would look in his bottom drawer and put everything that's in it into the gym bag sitting by his bed.

"I want you to take out like $3000 for yourself" Cream said, "leave me ten and hold the rest while I'm gone and oh yeah, can you put it in my truck for me too? There should be a extra set of keys on top of my dresser."

That was cool with Ray. You didn't have to tell him twice. If Cream asked Tymel to do something, he would probably still be on the phone explaining how and why. Ray would never give Simone the lowdown because she would have a fit and some things are best kept between men. Gunshots went off in the area daily, but this time since they sounded so close telling her what happened would only add stress.

"Tell Auntie I called and that I love her. Just say I went out of town and that I'll be back next week. If my mother calls tell her the same. You always come through for me Unk. I owe you one."

Ray didn't ask any questions at all before he hung up the phone. Twana knocked on the bathroom door after Cream hung up.

"I hope you didn't blow up the bathroom cause I got to use it," she said through the door.

"Now? I'll be out in a minute," Cream griped.

"Not now, but like right now. Open up."

Cream was taking a quick leak, but Twana opened the door before he was finished like she didn't care.

"I told you I'll be out in a minute" Cream huffed zipping up his jeans.

Twana was trying to see what he was doing and getting her peek on at the same time. Cream came out the bathroom pointing his thumb over his shoulder at Twana then shared the 411.

"You'll never guess who the driver was," Cream said staring up at the ceiling.

War didn't look too puzzled, but acted interested in knowing anyway.

"Mutha-fuckin' Bing-O," Cream divulged.

"Get the hell outta' here, Bing? I knew something was up with that cat." War laughed, with that sinister look in his eye.

Michelle seemed bored. She said she's had it with guys acting like they were gangsters all the time and was looking for something different.

"Yeah right Shell," Twana blurted after

flushing the toilet.

Cream got everyone's attention.

"This is what we're gonna' do," he said "I gotta' stop by my crib for a minute to get something. Then we're goin' to Ma'ati's spot so she can get a few things if she wants."

"We are?" Michelle inserted.

"Obviously" Ma'ati sighed, "we can't stay here Shell, if it's okay with you can Cream stay with us at your place tonight?"

"Can Warren come too?" War slipped in for himself.

"I don't know, I guess...but does this mean we're not going out like we planned?" Shell asked, a little irritated.

"Lets go then, it really stinks up in this rat hole," Twana complained, as if her number 2 odor didn't add to the room's mildewed funk.

"We out."

# Scene Sixteen

**Uncertain if anyone** reported Warren's plates or not, Cream suggested that Warren ditch his car just to be on the safe side. Warren didn't care, but nagged about just filling his gas tank, so Cream gave him the $20 deposit for returning the room key. They were only five minutes from the P.T Barnum housing project, which was like Father Panic's little brother. It was the perfect place to ditch a vehicle because PT was not just known for catching bodies, it was notorious for stripping cars left unattended for too long.

Shell drove extra slowly over the speed bumps following behind War. The P.T cats posted in the crevices of the red brick buildings, stared hard trying to see through the dark tint as they pulled over by the basketball courts. Before walking away from the chopped Maxima, Warren gathered the phony paperwork in the glove compartment, while Cream helped carry his CD's and tapes over to Shells ride.

"It's tight back here with three people baby, can you move them shiny legs over a bit?" Warren said, complaining that his nuts felt like tea bags.

Twana clamped her thigh master legs together now that she was in the middle of two big men in the backseat. She was fast for her age and took War's comment as a flirt. During the ride she would conveniently end up with her hand on his knee every time they stopped. Michelle kept looking at them through the rear view mirror sending messages with her eyes.

"*Act giddy if you want Warren, you can stay your ass in Bridgeport...and miss out on the real dea*l!" Shell's stare conveyed.

When they got to the Ave, Cream noticed that the homicide van was still parked on Clifford Street wrapping up their investigation. The beginning of Newfield Avenue was blocked off with yellow tape too, but luckily his Yukon was parked five cars down. He hopped out the Benz in front of Braxtons, stepping like everything was everything. Some nosy hood rats that witnessed the shootout were huddled off to the side eyeing his every move as he walked past them to get to his truck.

In the front sat a leather gym bag on the passenger floor containing some money in addition to a pistol and other personal items from Cream's room. Cream called uncle Ray to let him know he was out front.

"Just me again Unk...I got all the stuff, good looking out. Did you take out some money like I told you to?"

"Sure did. I took out three thousand like you said and I borrowed one more for the road. Don't worry about the rest it will be here when you get back."

"You got jokes," Cream started laughing, "It's all good though if my mother calls tell her I'm okay and I should visit soon. Give my love to Auntie and them and tell cuz I'ma see him. I'm outta' here."

"Be safe nephew."

Cream pulled off following Shell to Ma'ati's crib. When they arrived, the entire project looked desolate. Less than an hour ago the Tactical Narcotics Task Force (TNT) raided and arrested a busload of heads. Usually this only happened around election time, but there was a lot of political bullshit going on.

While Ma'ati and her sister went upstairs, Cream stood guard from the SUV. Twana and War stayed in the Benz parked along side of Cream so they could talk to each other from the window while they waited. Walking through the building some chickens tried screw facing Michelle cause her milkshake made all the thugs lamping in the lobby ogle as well.

"Do you know me?" Shell jeered as she walked past the hood boogers in the hallway, "you're staring like I owe you money bitch"

Ma'ati grabbed her sister's arm like she didn't have time for a catfight.

"They're just jealous, lets go" Ma'ati voiced, walking Shell into the elevator.

Michelle was the opposite of her sister. She was more out spoken, whereas Ma'ati kept her cool. Even so, a lot of men still found them both to be intimidating women.

"All they do is sit around waiting to start trouble like we used to do" Ma said, recalling all the fights they started back in the days.

As soon as they got inside the crib Ma'ati grabbed a few things out the closet. Shell made a few comments as Ma'ati counted out a couple thousand from a shoebox.

"I see Laquan was hitting you off lovely."

"The hell he was, forget Laquan! I'm not with him anymore. I told you that," Ma'ati retorted.

"Since when? You ain't tell me shit'!" Shell responded shocked.

"He tried to play me. Would you believe Jackie gave him head at the Jill Scott concert?"

"Oh my god for real! The same Jill Scott concert we all hit together?" Shell inquired.

"Kali told me your clique were backstabbers, but wait a minute," Shell sounded baffled, "how did she suck him off when we were all sitting next to each other?"

Ma'ati folded more clothes while looking up at her sister as she talked.

"Rememba' when Jackie went to the bathroom, then Laquan followed behind her to supposedly get drinks? Well...you know the rest. I only found out cause Riva was mad with Jackie...they go both ways you know, but anyway Riva ended up confessing everything she knew about Laquan and Jackie. So I confronted him about it and he didn't even deny it. I bumped into him when Cream took me to visit aunt Sherl and he said he still loves me and all this other crap. I was like please!" Ma brushed her shoulders off, "He thought he blew my mind but didn't even come close...you should've seen his face when I told him Cream was my new man Shell."

"Fuck Laquan's punk ass then! I'm hungry girl, let's go," Shell affirmed.

"You ain't hungry, who you kiddin'" Ma yelped, "You just wanna' get downstairs cause you think Warren is pushing up on Twana. I seen how you were eye balling him in the truck."

"True! I think he looks good! He's been approved for a prepaid pussy card. Did you see the size of his hands? He seems a lil' wild, but I like em' hard and rugged anyway," said Shell as she humped the bed.

The whole time the sisters were upstairs chitchatting, Warren and Cream were downstairs drilling Twana for information about her cousins. Twana revealed that Shell was a registered nurse and received the Benz as a gift from some big time drug dealer from around her way. She also told them that Ma'ati used to run the streets too, but wasn't really into the glamorous life as much as Shell was.

Cream looked curious as to what Ma'ati and her sister were so cheerfully discussing, when they came out of the building giggling hysterically. He had one arm hanging out the side of the window, while the other hand sat on his lap gripping his shiny .40 caliber just in case the beef came. Casually Ma'ati jumped in the truck with Cream instead of rolling with her sister.

After they left the Garden, Warren spent about five minutes in his mother's house gathering some cash and the rest of the product that he had left. He came out wearing a large beach towel over his head carrying a plastic thank you bag in his hand.

A 15-minute ride on I-95 north led them to Jimmy's Seafood restaurant in West Haven, CT after Shell complained that her stomach was growling from hunger. Essentially none of them had eaten anything all day, so they ordered tons of shrimp along with other side orders seated at the bar while waiting for a table.

When it came time for dinner, everyone was stuffed. The table of five had transferred their mound of horsd'oeuvres to a table facing a large bay window. The food was mediocre, but there was barely any dinner conversation out of the men, just sighs and grunts. For the most part the location was peaceful. The restaurant sat on beach property that overlooked Long Island Sound. A perfect setting for getting to know someone better.

Even though it was getting late, a warm breeze still lingered in the air. Warren asked Michelle if she would like to go outside with him, since she kept commenting about the New England scenery so much.

"You would never think Bridgeport was only fifteen-minutes away from here" she stated, "it's so serene."

As the two went outside, Ma'ati, Cream and Twana stayed seated in the restaurant. Twana felt out of place because her cousins were paired off with men and she wasn't. The hot in the ass outfit that she wore was a waste.

"I could've gone to City Island to eat with my nigga Ronny...this ain't all that you know! I knew I should've stayed home" she wined.

"Oh will you stop it Twana, you're the one that begged to come with us remember? Fall back Miss thing...you don't need to get any more cute than you already are."

After sharing a fake smile with Ma'ati, Twana sat there looking at her nails talking shit under her breath as Ma carried on with the conversation.

"So what's all this talk about businesses? I know I'm nosy, but I overheard you and War talkin'?

"You don't miss a beat do you? We were just politicking about investments. I don't know about him, but I'm tired of the B.S. I'm ready to take my self to the next level nah'mean?"

Twana became bored with the insightful conversation and went outside. Ma'ati mentioned to Cream that if he was serious, they could hook up on the business tip and get some powerful things accomplished together.

"So what DO you do Ma?" He intrusively asked.

"Well lets just say I used to run a cleaning service, but the employees decided to go into business for themselves" Ma'ati answered.

Cream slid closer to Ma with every syllable that came out of her mouth. They shared a couple of ideas about businesses that could add on, instead of those that subtracted like most establishments in the hood. As an overview of reality when it came to black owned business it was truly monotonous! With all the diverse things in life, you would think people would establish different types of businesses, but there were barbershops and beauty salons on every corner. Some seem to forget that ANY type of business In the world can be a black owned one.

Eventually the copycat establishments cancel each other out after competing to the death. If its not that, customers that patronize black business always want "hook-ups" and feel that they're not as respectable as other businesses. Between the lack of creativity and the lack of knowledge that so called black entrepreneurs possess, establishing a business with longevity in the hood is almost impossible. The complexity to get paid, while at the same time restoring balance is the conundrum.

# Scene Seventeen

**Ma'ati started to tell** Cream something important then lowered her voice like she changed her mind.

"Sisters like me are dangerous to the game cause I know its all an illusion. Compulsory education is and always has been an instrument of warfare. So for me it's all about raising the consciousness and freeing minds."

Cream didn't catch "the sisters like me" part. The waitress distracted him while she cleared the table. He paid the bill then walked Ma'ati out of the restaurant onto the pier.

Shell sat freely, watching the waves crash against the rocks with her feet dug in the sand alongside of Warren who was throwing pebbles at the seagulls. They were getting along just like Ma'ati thought they would. Twana on the other hand, was acting a fool backing in and out of empty parking spaces with her cousin's G5.

"Where you think you at, the Cayman Islands?" Cream posed as he stood on the boardwalk looking down at War and Shell.

Warren put his shirt back on with Shells help and they took the long way around the pier. Up until Ma'ati turned around to walk away, Cream hadn't noticed that she was wearing a captivating top with the back out. Inside the restaurant the air conditioning was on full blast, so she kept her jacket on the entire time. As she walked away, Cream found himself gawking once again. Ma definitely filled out her skirt, which made the top of her thong show a little as her cheeks moved up and down left to right.

"*Those only come in black!*" He thought to himself referring to the shapely cheeks he desired to palm and slap up against.

Passing between two parked vehicles, Cream spun Ma'ati around so they could look at each other face to face.

"I can't hold it in anymore, I think you got it goin' on sweetness and I would love to get with you. I'm not gonna' front either, when we first met I was attracted to you physically...who wouldn't be your body's off the hook, but a woman who thinks like you by my side is what I need. You're the total package I asked to be delivered."

Cream looked up at the sky folding his hands like he was thanking the heavens as Ma'ati laughed pleasantly.

"And I want to make it officially known that if you accept my offer of establishing a more intimate relationship, I would want to exclusively share our time together and..."

"Cream baby, slow down you sound like a lawyer. That's mad sweet boo boo, I feel you like that and everything too, but...there's a lot of things you don't know about me."

"Before you say anything else," Cream said, placing his large hands on her waist, "I just wanna' say that together I think we can build a foundation that we can both stand on."

Ma'ati was some what wooed from the way

he came at her. She let go of all doubt closing her eyes and just as Cream went to kiss her, Twana blew up the spot by annoyingly beeping the horn.

"Baap! Baap! Baap! Baap!"

"You ain't havin' me out here all night by myself like a herb," she shouted from the SUV, "I'm ready to go!

Ma'ati and Cream stared at Twana like the buster that she was. Ignoring her jealous whimpering, they embraced into a tight hug and ended it with a long wet frenchy. That's when Warren came up behind the two lovebirds carrying Shell on his back. Michelle smiled, noticing how cute her little sister looked hugged up with the brawny and handsome looking Cream.

"I thought you were ready to bounce?" War asked.

"We are now, thanks!" Cream answered.

"Before we hit the city can we stop at a friend's house real quick?" Warren asked Shell, "He's holding some money for me that's all,"

Shell was happy enough to let Twana drive even though she didn't have her license yet. Swerving through traffic, they arrived in Greenwich, CT in a half-hour. The ghetto fabulous Yukon Denali and G500 Mercedes Benz were like hoop rides in Greenwich, compared to all the Bentleys people drove around in. Unlike Bridgeport, the streets were meticulous without a piece of trash in sight. The lampposts were even stained with real gold leaf and each home they passed sat on acres of land with horse stables on the properties.

"See if I was hustlin' I would set up shop around this muthafucka'" Twana expressed, "find me a punk ass white girl to slap around...shit. I'll have her ass slinging keys up in these mansions. I don't know what the deal is with you Snitch-port niggas, but it looks like the big boy cash is out here!"

"Just take a left right here gangsta' girl," War instructed.

Twana pulled into the circled driveway where cars were parked all over the place like a party was going on. The landscaper turned off his lawnmower to hear what his boss was screaming at him.

"PEDRO! Turn that goddamn thing off right now!" he chastised, "I can hardly hear myself think. I thought I told you to trim the hedges, not mow the fucking lawn!"

Rupert hollered at Pedro like he was his slave. The hardworking Mexican just walked away with his head down in an obedient manner. Dressed in a salmon-colored sweater with a doo-rag on his head, Rupert walked over to the truck like he was George Jefferson swinging his arms behind his back.

"Hey the homies arrived! Are you feeling my crib B? I am so gangster right?"

Shell looked at Warren like you actually know this asshole?

"Yo you got the fuckin' money or what?" Warren hollered, hopping out embarrassed.

He intimidated the spoiled white boy by pulling him away from the truck then pushing Rupert to go ahead of him as his cell rang.

"Serve this clown so we can bounce" Cream said, then hung up.

While Warren had a team in the Garden selling rocks for him, he was fashioning new clientele selling Oxycotin. Tootsie had so much of it to steal because she worked in a Stamford manufacturing plant that produced the opium based prescription drug. Oxy was said to offer a greater high than heroin and cravers of the prescription drug peeled off the coating, crushed it into a powder then sniffed it. Warren even tried it once, but his lust for money and fame was much more addictive.

The huge mansion was filled with people laid out all over the place. A skinny topless blonde was sniffing a line of Ox off some guy's erection at the same time another couple poured wax on each other's privates. War stood around checking the peculiar party out, while Rupert went to gather more money from his friends. His parents weren't the average rich white people either. His father who was on vacation in Switzerland with his 22-year-old tennis instructor, owned record labels and television stations. His mother was on vacation too, with her young Swedish psychiatrist in Hawaii.

Warren's desire to rob and tie up each and every one of the spoiled drug addicted brats, grew as they continued to party. Before he even arrived Rupert seemed jittery and after noticing the pistol in Warren's waistband his nervousness increased as he walked down the stairs counting money.

"You got lice or somethin'? Stop scratching your damn head, matter of fact take that fuckin' Doo-rag off!"

War pulled the senseless headgear off, throwing it to the floor before snatching the roll of Benjamin's out of his hand. Rupert hurriedly tested the Oxy for substance by doing a line off his hand.

"Becky told me this shit's the bomb" he took another sniff, "Count it man, I would never play you dood."

War tossed him a bundle of crack too, then walked out the door counting the money. Of course he overcharged Rupert like he did Becky. It didn't matter cause mommy and daddy would just give him more cash when they got back anyway.

Twana was standing outside of the truck near the water fountain smoking a cig, then sat on one of the Ducati motorcycles parked on the property playfully revving the throttle. Rupert followed War out the door fixing his belt buckle, while he stared at Twana like he had a thing for black girls.

"Dood is that one of your hoes? I bet she would do anything to live in a place like this...hook me up my nig...?"

"WHAPP!" Warren back handedly slapped the drug boogers out of Rupert's nose then punched him in the face.

"Please don't kill me! Please! I'm down. I'm down! Stop kicking me, help Pedro do something!" Rupert whimpered for help.

War motioned for Twana to come over to them.

"What's up?" Twana inquired, looking down at Rupert lying there like a pile of dung.

"Nothing I can't handle" War replied, "Eminem over here thought you was a trick. You said you we're looking for a lil' bitch to slap around, and he sits down to piss, so go ahead and rep yo hood."

Twana didn't hesitate at all. She bent over and slapped Rupert like a silly hooker.

"I'm not your nigga either punk!" War kicked, "just tell all your friends who got the good shit white boy and most of all, never disrespect my company *dood*!"

"I know you got more money on you, you cherry face muthafucka!" Twana snapped, while she patted down Rupert's pockets for more loot.

After she took off his shoes and socks, Twana stomped his lips then kicked him in his nuts as he attempted to stand up.

"Shut the fuck up" she said, gritting her teeth before kicking him in the groin one last time.

With a bloody nose screaming like a little girl, Rupert stayed on the ground with his hands in his pants curled up like a baby as the pair of SUV's drove off the premises. The exploited Mexican sat on the John Deere cracking up. He wasn't getting involved in shit. Rupert demanded his help repeatedly, but Pedro got the last laugh by starting the lawn mower like he couldn't hear a thing.

# Scene Eighteen

**Slouched in the passenger seat** chillin', Warren placed his hand over the headrest. Twana gave him palm like she was one of his boys from the block then continued to count the couple of hundred she got off Rupert.

"I know that guy acted like a dick, but what did he say to make you kick him like that?"

Warren never answered, so Shell asked her cousin the same thing. Twana was $800 richer. She just laughed blowing Shell off too, then began talking about what she was going to buy and who was going to be jealous after seeing her wearing it.

When they got to the city they stopped Uptown first to drop Twana off. She lived in the Polo Grounds, but got out four blocks from her building after seeing some of her girls coming out of Moreno's Market.

"You can drop me off right here okay Shell? I'm gonna' roll with my click."

"Don't use me as an excuse to hang out all night Twana. Make sure you tell your mother what time I brought you home cause I don't want auntie cursing me out again," Shell stressed.

"Bye...War-ren" Twana uttered slowly.

From the way she licked her lips it appeared as if she wanted to get with him.

"Ai'ight shorty, be good" War replied, winking his eye on the low after secretly sliding her his number.

Twana stepped away from the Benzo like it was her hood debut. She shook her hips real extra, trying to entice Warren with a lasting image. Cream was parked right behind Shell, so Ma'ati got out to give her cousin a hug goodbye.

"You can call me if you need anything okay? I'm sorry if I've been a lil' ruff toward you Twana. I just want you to take your time coming up. You're speedin' girl. It's crazy out here and these streets can swallow you whole...just be safe okay?"

Twana still acted funny like she didn't need to be told nothing about nothin'.

It's all good Tiara holla'!" Twana enunciated.

In her straight out of Harlem disposition, Twana waved her cousins off as they U-turned down Broadway.

There was so much to get into. Shell exited the West Side Highway heading for her apartment in the Bowery section, while Warren rapped over the radio releasing pent up energy. He felt like getting his club on and so did Shell. The sisters were already dressed for a night out on the town and had plans to go clubbing before they even ran into Cream and Warren anyway. Friday nights in New York City would certainly remind anyone that the world don't stop spinning for nobody!

In most of lower Manhattan living in a run down looking facade was chic. The outside of Shell's apartment building looked like an abandoned warehouse, but inside however the place could have made the pages of Architectural Digest. To get inside the lavish loft you could either take the former factory staircase or use the classic freight elevator. Warren went with Shell upstairs, while Cream and Ma waited in the truck given that Shell said they would be back in a minute.

"What took you so long? Did you forget we were out here," Ma chided when they finally came back fifteen minutes later.

She suspected Shell and Warren were fooling around cause they were touchy-feely getting into Cream's Yukon. Disappointingly enough the men weren't dressed for the type of clubs that the girl's had in mind because they enforced strict dress codes, like no jeans, no hats or sneakers. There were some regular bars that they could get into Michelle stated, but they had no dance floor. After flirting all day Shell was dying to see how Warren danced to get a better idea of how he moved in bed. Ma'ati spoke up acknowledging that she knew a place that was off the hook without a specific dress code and said she even knew some of the bouncers that worked there.

"Are you sure this is it?" Cream asked five minutes later as they convened on the South Street Seaport pier.

The line waiting on the dock was bananas! There was only ten minutes to board the three level boat club before it pulled out to the Hudson.

"You can slide in front of me baby doll" some dude in line wolf called, as Ma'ati strolled toward the front.

Shell grabbed her sister's hand pulling her past some guys that were checking them out from the front of the line.

"*You and that booty always got a space on my face baby*," one uttered making shrill noises.

The cornballs didn't seem to mind two sexy ladies cutting in front of them, until Cream and

Warren burst their bubbles by sliding in between. None of them dared address any dissatisfaction as Cream stared them down like he would punch their whole crew in the face if they had any problems.

Michelle loved the attention, even more so when men were going to fight over her. A bit thicker than her sister, Shell had cantaloupe size breasts whereas Ma'ati was in the mango category. When it came to the back though, Ma'ati was holding much much more cake.

"That's it for tonight ladies and gentleman," the bouncer boisterously announced, even though his tight shirt looked like it was constricting his breath.

The crowds of people left standing in line were pissed. The last two people to board the party boat were Shell and Ma'ati. After they whispered something in the bouncer's ear he lifted the rope letting their two dates aboard. War and Cream were thoroughly searched probably more so than others, because they were dressed like teenagers wearing fitted caps and throwbacks. As the boat pulled away, people left stranded on the dock could be seen arguing with each other for letting Ma and them cut.

Club Float On had it popping. The jump off was about to be jumped off. There were three levels to choose from. Rap on the first floor, Dancehall on the bottom and Club music on the third. There was a main bar on the first floor, but each level had its own mini bars.

"Who got the first round" War hollered over the loud music as they made their way to the bar, "you treatin' boo?" He nudged Shell.

To everyone's surprise Ma'ati began ordering drinks for everyone.

"Two bottles of Red Alize' please" She requested, handing the bartender a hundred-dollar bill. She wasn't a big time drinker herself and was basically ordering the bottles for the fella's.

"Make that one Alize' and a bottle of Hennessy instead," Cream cut in.

The bartender frowned like there was a problem. He said that only Champaign and Alize' were sold by the bottle.

"How does an extra fifty sound?"

Money talks. The bartender put the $50 up to the light to check its authenticity then folded it into his shirt pocket. Cream handed War the Henny, while he carried the ice bucket and Alize' over to a table.Since everyone was on the dance floor doing it up, most of the tables were available.

After Warren mixed the bottles into a thug passion, Shell led him by the wrist down to the Reggae floor to rub a dub. Weed smoke blew through the air stronger than any women's perfume. With both hands in the air Shell winded her waist like she was slowly belly dancing. Warren joined in from behind with his left hand in the air, drinking straight from the bottle. Next to them were a few older folks moving like those mechanical dancing Santas.

It only took a few seconds of grinding on Shell's soft body for Warren to become erect. Warren got so hard that he had to fix his stiffness into the waistband of his jeans so people wouldn't notice his bulge. He had pre-cum all over his stomach. Shell was working her dance moves so hard that they ended up in a corner backed against a wall. She placed her hands on War's shoulders then ran them down his rigid chest. When Shell got to Warren's abs, she took a surprising step back.

"*I know I seen him get checked at the door*? Shell thought to herself.

"Oh my god!" Shell lifted up Warren's jersey then bust out laughing, "No he didn't!" She uttered in shock.

Still in awe of the situation, she lifted his jersey again to get a second look. Shell seemed more turned on now than before.

"Look at that thing! It's throbbing like my heart is right now. You had me scared for a minute cause I thought you snuck a gun in here!"

Upstairs Ma'ati and Cream were stepping in the name of love. The DJ was rocking the turntables, switching records in the middle of the songs then bringing them back.

"*Step, step, side to side...*" sounded from the speakers.

When he mixed *Touch Me Tease Me* by *Case* with *In Da Club*, the dance floor shifted even harder. The crowd shouted along with the music, *"Go shorty, it's ya birthday...Go shorty, it's ya birthday...we don't give a fuck it's not ya' birthday*!"

After spending hours tearing up the dance floor Shell wiped the sweat from her brow deciding to take a cigarette break. She didn't smoke that often, but whenever she drank alcohol the urge appeared. She found Ma'ati then they stepped outside onto the bow. Cream and Warren headed for the unisex restroom.

Shell bummed a cigarette from a girl smoking nearby then tapped her sister on the arm.

"Girl let me ask you something where did you find these niggas? Warren is buck! Yo he's enough! I'm dancing right, doing my thang, you know how I do, when all of a sudden I felt this rock hard dick sticking in his waistband like he was carrying a pistol. Ma...that shit had to be like a foot long! It was all the way up his stomach," she yelped.

"Stop it Shell you lyin'," Ma'ati chuckled along with the rest of the women standing next to them giggling like little schoolgirls.

While Michelle told her sister everything that happened, a sea sick chick throwing up off the side of the boat thought that they were making fun of her, because everyone kept laughing at the way Shell told the humorous account.

"How are you and Raheem doin'?" Shell asked, imitating Cream's deep voice.

"I don't kiss n' tell, but I felt pokes in my back all night," Ma'ati conceded.

"You know what girl...I wanna' get me some tonight. I mean I would fuck him on the humble anyway, but you don't know...War got me wetter than the water we're floating on," Michelle confessed after taking a long drag of the cancer stick.

Ma'ati was feeling a little horny too. She hadn't had any sex since she broke up with Laquan. She pulled the cigarette out of her sister's mouth flicking it over board before pushing her back inside the club.

"I almost bust off in my pants from the way Shell was grinding on me!" Warren communicated with Cream between the stalls.

Cream hollered back, "you ain't sayin' nothin' kid. The way me and Ma were freaking it Shell might be my sister-in-law soon."

Warren had a harem of hoes and wasn't thinking about building a relationship like Cream. He just wanted to fuck. They both just laughed flushing the toilets at the same time.

The lights throughout the club flashed three times signaling the party people that the boat would be docking in 10 minutes. Sweaty bodies wobbled through the exit flooding the pier, as Club Float On finally docked.

Ma'ati was the only one who could remember where they parked. She didn't drink as heavy as everyone else did and decided that it was best if she drove home. Naturally Warren and Shell didn't complain cause they could flirt in the backseat.

"I got somethin' delicious for you if you're that hungry baby?" Shell whispered to Warren after he mentioned how much he was starving.

Ma'ati overheard the conversation and smiled in the rear view. She wouldn't mind Cream's full lips feasting on her honey bun either. When they arrived home, Shell quickly concluded the evening by stretching her arms like she was totally exhausted.

"Well...I think I'm gonna' call it a night" she yawned, inadvertently letting out a tipsy hiccup, "A woman must get her booty *oops*, I mean beauty sleep."

Warren didn't say goodnight or anything else, he just followed Shell up the spiral staircase onto a split-level platform, which led to her bedroom. Seconds later a sliding screen opened from upstairs. Two pillows and a big fluffy comforter came dropping down on Cream's head as he sat on Michelle's modish Workbench furniture. Since they were going out of business, Shell got it for 60% off.

"Not only is it a couch" Shell intoxicatingly bellowed from above, "it's also pull out bed so enjoy."

Ma'ati had already taken off her shoes and started to massage her toes to relieve some of the stress that her feet endured all day and night.

"Why don't you come over here suga' so I can help you with that," Cream eagerly proposed.

His offer was kindly accepted. Ma'ati plopped down next to him with no delay. She laid back, allowing Cream to work his magical hands all over her pretty feet, toes and ankles.

Things were heating up in Shells room too. Warren was already naked standing at the foot of the bed already. Shell clapped her hands to adjust the lighting, since she had one of those clapper modules that turn the lights off and on. Undressing slowly, she only left her choker necklace and low-heeled shoes on that she wore to the club. Warren's manhood sprung to attention like a diving board after witnessing Shell's delectable E-cups drop in the shadow's silhouette.

"Bring that chocolate pole over here so I can tame that big ole' monster," commanded Shell subsequent to clapping the lights back on. She wanted to see every inch of Warren before things got real freaky.

About 14 feet below, Cream was downstairs lying on his stomach with his shirt off and jeans on.

"Damn baby, did you get caught cheating on the wrong chick or something?" Ma'ati asked, as she sat on his back examining the old bullet scars that tattooed his shoulder blade.

"Nah I'm too smooth for that, but you should see the otha' nigga. I was lucky though cause a couple of inches lower would've hit my heart."

Ma'ati gently kissed the back of Cream's neck then licked the shape of his ear moving her tongue down the side of his chin. Cream was loving it, but couldn't take much more. He stopped what she was doing so he could finally undress her. Ma'ati's top came off effortlessly being that only a string tied around her neck held it together. He took a second to admire the beauty Ma'ati exuded, tenderly tweaking her pencil eraser top nipples into complete rigidity.

He continued to lick them lavishly as Ma'ati was left to pant in submission. She felt all over Cream's chiseled out chest digging her nails into his chocolate pecks. After Ma'ati's skirt dropped to the floor Cream surprisingly placed his forearms between her legs gripping both of her luscious butt cheeks from up under as he lifted Ma'ati to his face. She seemed to be light as a feather. Cream then carefully pulled her cherry thong to the side with his teeth and as Ma'ati's moans increased he intensified his tongue's slithering pressure against her clitoris.

"Oh shee_it" Ma'ati groaned, gripping on Cream's cornrows as he washed his face between her clamped thighs.

She emitted a low cry high in the air with her back arched against the wall, squeezing Cream's head between her legs in total ecstasy. After Ma'ati's first orgasm he flipped her upside down into a standing 69 position. She abruptly unbuckled his belt causing his jeans to fall to his ankles gasping for air while she fit him into her mouth.

Five minutes later Cream tossed her onto the convertible bed. Ma'ati grabbed Cream's thick shaft introducing his dick to the most steaming hot pussy he had ever stabbed. As Cream thrust with rotation, Ma'ati pumped it back the same flexing her Kegel muscles to generate the feeling of a hand inside her vagina tightly milking his penis. Once they switched positions she began riding him backwards like a professional jockey, bringing about a synchronized climax. It didn't even matter that the pull out bed was squeaky, because upstairs the lights were turning off and on from the slapping sounds that Warren and Shell were making doing it doggy style.

# Scene Nineteen

**What started as a weekend sleepover**, had turned into a zesty three-week vacation full of sex, shopping and dinning out. Warren was up early this morning fixing breakfast again, but of course after he and Shell snuck a quickie in the shower. All week he showed off the cooking skills he acquired upstate, while doing an 18-month prison stint for illegal discharge of a firearm. It was there in the Osborn Correctional Institution where Warren had first met Bing-O and Geek.

Shell came out of the bathroom wearing a knee length Sponge Bob tee shirt to cover her Vickie secret panties. Ma was still knocked out on the convertible lying next to Cream under the covers.

"Wake up sleepy head, my boo boo made us breakfast. Come on, get up Ma'ati," Shell nagged shaking her sister's leg.

Ma'ati opened her eyes, slicing into Shell with a dirty look.

"I'm up yo, I am up! Will you stop grabbing my leg with those ice cold hands!"

"Forget you then" Shell stuck out her tongue, "that's why your breath smells like dick!"

She was only joking cause like usual Ma'ati's breath was plum sweet this morning. Cream tossed and turned after the covers were suddenly pulled off.

"Looks like you had fun again last night too," Shell murmured walking away with a thick body switch.

"You're so nasty Shell, stop!" Ma'ati laughed, throwing a pillow at her sister for peeking at the tent pitched in Cream's boxers.

Shell and Warren had mad sex jokes during breakfast conversation. Cream let the two hecklers know that he heard them this morning when he tried to use the bathroom. Even though Shell was chocolate it was easy to see her blushing. It was all love though, but Warren tried embarrassing Ma'ati to get back at Cream for getting on Shell.

"Look who's talking, I seen that condom on the floor by the couch. Don't try to front like y'all wasn't gettin' busy."

Ma'ati spoke up in her own defense after taking a large bite of the peach that she was wiping off while they gossiped.

"There's no shame in my game kid, I'm grown...wha' what. Seriously though, I don't know whose hat that is. I'm scared to use condoms after the shit I found out. And definitely not those lubricated joints. It must be one of Shell's.

"Word Ma?" Warren's eyes jumped back in his head, "you don't use protection, why not?" he asked.

Needless to say Cream knew that already. Ma'ati kept on eating her fruit, crackling her toes and stretching her legs.

"Hello Tiara...safe sex...STD's...AIDS!"

Ma'ati played it cool than answered her sister's apprehensive remarks. "You're lookin' at me like I'm nasty or somethin' Shell. I keep my kitty kat immaculate. Inside and out."

"Yeah it's so clean you can eat off of it," Cream threw in.

"All jokes aside Shell, you know I want the best for me and mines, but I found out some crazy shit about condoms that most people probably didn't hear yet. So let me break it down for you since you don't read the newsletters that your job mails you."

Ma'ati sat down and began to expound about her peculiar statement about safe sex.

"First off, you should all know by now cause it's not a secret anymore that AIDS was a man made biological weapon. An insidious political group had to convince the constituency at some point that the original way of 'doin' it' wasn't safe anymore and that we needed a barrier between us during intercourse."

"People been fuckin' without condoms since the beginning of time" Cream butt in after warren uttered something silly, "what are you talkin' about son, how do you think you were conceived?"

"Will you two let me talk for a minute... damn! Anyway when you study the Nixon administration you'll find out that about thirty-three years ago President Richard M. Nixon signed a public law (91-213) that authorized, get this, population stabilization. He feared the overpopulation of Non-whites worldwide. Soon after that shit millions of dollars were allocated to create a Special Virus program to deal with population control."

Everyone in the room seemed interested, but looked sort of lost.

"Come on now, what do you think population control is!" Ma exclaimed, "It's either killing people or stopping babies from being born! It didn't take long before the same people who thought the world needed a population reduction, produced a cancer-causing agent along with a huge misinformation campaign about so called 'protection and safe sex'. Nixon appointed John D. Rockefeller, who spent his life engaged in the racist ideology of eugenics, to oversee this population issue. Check it out for yourselves."

"So what does that have to do with not using protection Tiara!"? Shell sounded frustrated and confused. She always strapped up...well most times she did and had much concern to learn more.

"Everything sis!" Ma'ati replied, "it's in the condom."

"So how do we protect ourselves then?" Warren asked, confused about the situation too.

"Get a gun! No, seriously...think about what you asked like this Warren, mobsters used to extort big money from local business and call it protection when obviously what they were doing was straight up extortion. What you call protection doesn't necessarily protect you at all. Think about the kind of rubbers they always give out for free or insist that we use. Shell's work memo even warns that any contraceptive with Nonoxynol-9 on it increases your chances of developing HIV/AIDS. And I bet you that the Nonoxynol-9 shit is the same cancer-causing chemical that those population control fanatics developed. And condoms don't stop herpes or crabs anyway so what'chu talkin' bout Warren?"

Ma'ati remained firm in her controversial findings, while Cream added his thoughts to the perplexity of the whole thing.

"That shit's wild. Kill two birds with one

stone. The noxious condom would help lower the pregnancy rate and increase the death rate at the same time, its brilliant if you wanna' kill a bunch of muthafucka's..." he reflected vocally, "Yo!!" Cream roared.

"Damn man that's my ear!" War spat out.

"Chill, chill. Remember in history class when they taught us about the Trojan horse," Cream brought to mind.

"Nah I think I skipped that one," War rejoined.

"Well the Trojan horse was a giant wooden horse that the Greeks built as a gift. They gave it to their rivals the Trojans, since they had a hard time beating them or getting through their colossal defensive gateway. So in their sneaky conquest the Greeks acted like they wanted to end the beef. As a token of new friendship they gave the Trojans the giant horse offering. Unknown to the Trojans, the Greeks had soldiers laid up in the horse and after they let them through the gates, the Greek soldiers burst out of it, killing the people of Troy and lastly defeating their enemies. If the Trojans didn't willingly except a gift from their adversary they would have never been defeated. Notice any similarities?" Cream asked as he held the condom up in the air with a Trojan print on It.

Michelle couldn't believe what she was hearing. As a registered nurse who studied a little medicine, she had never heard talk like this about HIV/AIDS, despite the fact that she watched her uncle deteriorate, after he started taking so called treatment for the ghastly disease.

"I know I'm not a doctor Shell, but ever since uncle Byron died, I've been studying this AIDS thing as much as I could. I'm just telling you what the deal is sis, cause I love you. Your newsletter declared that women are at high-risk cause Nonoxynol-9 irritates the womb and supposedly causes cervical cancer, which by the way is under the umbrella of HIV. Check it out for yourself Shell, you got access to more information than me. You should be able to download some of the things I'm talkin' about on the American Health Consultants website AHCPub.com, check it out whenever you decide to go back to work."

"You're too deep for me girl," Shell exhaled a long breath as she sat on the couch.

Ma'ati retained the teachings that their father taught them, which was to analyze their findings and form a conclusion based on their own consciousness. He taught them to never forget that all history is a current event and if you don't keep up with it, he said, you'll just keep getting played. It's not about reading books and repeating what's read, rather research your information and compare notes for yourself, he cultured.

A couple of hours went by carrying on with more deep conversation as they all lounged in the living room watching TV.

"So you're saying that the same Rockefeller family we were just talking about owns Roc-A-Fella records?"

"Who knows...the Rockefellers own Standard Oil, which share the same flame symbol for a logo. Their other company, Amoco even has the torch and flame."

"Oh shit!" Shell shouted, "look, Laquan's picture is on TV!"

*"Police found the body of an up and coming Rap star Laquan Brown, lead vocalist in the gangster rap group Phonetic Doom, early*

*yesterday morning in his Brooklyn apartment. Reports also say that four other men were found at the scene. All five victims suffered gunshot wounds to the head. Foul play is suspected. Brown was the sixth rapper killed this month. AND IN OTHER NEWS...*" Cream turned off the television.

Ma'ati had a blank look on her face, stunned that her ex-boyfriend had been murdered and they showed it on TV. Her eyes became watery and her leg was nervously shaking up and down. Cream wiped a tear from her eye tracing Ma's mouth with his finger to console her somewhat then kissed her on the forehead to soothe the somber news.

Ma'ati was saddened, but more shocked than anything. She was truly mournful for Laquan's mother whom she got along with really well. As far as Shell was concerned, Laquan treated her sister like shit, but she still felt remorse because he was still once a person in her sister's life.

Suddenly the phone rang. It was Vivian, Twana's mother, concerned about her daughter's whereabouts since she hadn't come home again last night. Vivian wondered if Twana was still with Shell and them.

"I knew she was going to pull that shit again! I should've dropped her butt off home," Shell declared over the phone.

The day before yesterday Shell drove Twana to a community health clinic for a summer job interview and felt responsible cause she took her there. *But Twana is 16 she thought, which is too old to be held by the hand and walked through life*. Shell suspected her little cousin was probably hanging out around Rucker Park somewhere. Twana would usually break night with her friends, slowly working her way home building by building.

"Twana's father is coming down today," Vivian acknowledged, "so if you happen to see my hard head child Shell, can you tell her what I said?"

"Its not a problem auntie Viv."

Before Shell hung up she promised her aunt that she'd make it a priority to drive Uptown to look for Twana after she got dressed.

On a brighter note, the sun was beaming. For the last couple of weeks it had been cool outside being summer and all, but today it really looked and felt like July. Cream and Warren took no time at all getting dressed. Their gear was always simple. Clean white XXL tee shirts, baggy jeans and Timbs. Warren chose to display his defined shape-up, while Cream rocked a doo-rag under his Baltimore Black Sox fitted cap.

The sisters, on the other hand, took a little bit more time getting ready. Michelle always rocked designer clothes, nothing fugayzi either. The material bug had bit her a long time ago. She slid into her orange satin Louis Vuitton dress with a pair of black Sergio Rossi cutout thong boots that had orange stitching to match the color of her dress. The diamond stud earrings that she adjusted in her ears, flashed like strobe lights each time she walked past the sunrays shining through the large loft windows.

After rubbing herself down with peppermint lotion, Ma'ati threw on a custom pair of stretch jeans that were completely cut up the sides. They exposed the tone of her thighs with only five extra large safety pins on each side to hold them together. To make her outfit fully unique she wore an Earth Wind & Fire tee shirt that she stylishly turned into a halter-top in her spare time. Considering how diamonds were horrendously exploiting African children in Sierra Leone who died mining the excessively cherished stones, Ma'ati stopped flossing ice and wore an appealing amethyst bracelet.

"Are my shades and cell on the kitchen table?" Shell asked whoever listened.

"Yeah they're right here" War answered.

He handed her the rimless orange tint Dolce & Gabana sunglasses and now they were officially ready to go. Warren felt like stuffing his fist in his mouth seeing Shell work it in her outfit. Ma'ati wasn't name branded out, but looked just as hot as Shell did. Keeping her promise to head Uptown in search of Twana, Shell drove with one arm hanging out the side of her Benz feeling the summer breeze.

# Scene Twenty

**Back in Bridgeport** things were still out of hand. The city Police Commissioner, Bruno Garliano had a daunting awakening when informed that his brother and business partner was arrested Friday night. Ironically Bruno was scared he'd end up behind bars like Mayor Ganim. His brother Sammy Garliano was initially indicted for child molestation including sodomy and rape, after a shocking home video involving the politician and other well-known bureaucrats on the city council, leaked into the public domain. The tape showed them having anal sex with minors during one of Sammy's infamous pool parties. While serving the warrants, Sammy was later charged with numerous counts of drug possession with intent to sell after officers found a substantial amount of Ecstasy in his home.

Ma'ati's best friend Kali was the one who mailed the tape to the local press as well as to some of the Garliano's political rivals, knowing that they'd have a field day with it. Character assassination was only the first step in bringing down the Garlianos because Kali always paid her targets with the reciprocity they deserved.

In some cities they say that the mob runs the drug business, but in Bridgeport that wasn't entirely true. Italians were never known for moving weight in the Bang Bang. They actually ran things like construction contracts and worker's unions. Being that a mob-like figure was heading the city's police department, they only regulated the drug game by enforcing and accepting payoffs from dealers. Don't be fooled by movies and rap lyrics, in the streets anybody can get it...mob connected or not.

Kali in company with Ma'ati, came to town to shake shit up. Kali got close to the Garlianos by dating one of Bruno's number one snitches. But whenever Dirty Roy brought her around the crooked cops and slippery politicians, they played her close. Nobody suspected that she was up to anything, it was just procedure to separate the employees from the bosses. And they definitely didn't suspect Kali as being the daughter of a celebrated vigilante.

For federal agents working with the government program known as *Operation Black Sweep*, it was no big surprise that the Garliano campaign was running a corrupt organization. The FEDS never moved on the Garlianos, because they had orders not to do so. After Internal Affairs viewed the videotape, they were forced to raid Sammy's Westport, CT home to save face. Between the myriad of child pornography found on his computer's hard drive and the massive amount of drugs seized, public officials could no longer turn their heads the other way either.

Like any other inner city in the country, Bridgeport was targeted for gentrification. The purpose of *Operation Black Sweep* was to help speed up the process. It purposely infected sections of the city that had profitable real estate potential with crack cocaine, cheap heroin and potent marijuana. This same covert operation was also responsible for the over crowded prisons and excessive murder rate the city suffered over the years.

The Drug "Enforcement" Agency cataloged felons convicted on drug charges for a period of fifteen years, choosing particular inmates to work the streets for them once they've finished doing their bids. The actual word "Enforcement" means to insist or impose, thus the DEA lived up to its name supplying the streets with drugs, rather than taking them off the street.

Other objectives of *Operation Black sweep* were to disrupt organization in the hood. If the growing number of cash stacking, gun toting drug dealers organized into legitimate operations, the powers that be were scared that their influence and control of the city would lessen if they didn't co-opt things first. So counter-intelligence units were assigned.

Every gang in Bridgeport was targeted. After Black Sweep flooded the streets with undercover agents and snitches, it was only a short period of time before the gang's established code of ethics crumbled. Albeit, underground crews like the Body Snatchers, BushMobb, Madd Brothers, Foundation, Brotherhood and Nation dudes, kept it gangster in spite of the counter intelligence assigned to monitor their activity. Organizations like the Latin Kings were also saturated tremendously with agents and were soon brought to national attention as proof that more federal funding was needed to stop gangs from taking over prison and the streets.

Dirty Roy, the leader of the SOS posse, an acronym for the "Shoot em' On Sight posse" was Bruno Garliano's main link to Bridgeport's underworld. Roy Carter AKA Dirty Roy had moved dope for years under Garliano's control and paid a fortune in payoffs. Roy was popped in a buy & bust sting some time ago and rather than do the six month jail sentence, he became Bruno "the no neck" Garliano's bitch. At the time Bruno was only head of the Narcotics division and hadn't received his commissioner title yet. Roy's relationship with the police was not such an odd thing because corruption was always prevalent in Bridgeport. It just seemed to skyrocket ever since the suburbs merged with the inner city drug trade.

Dirty Roy sat absentminded in Bruno's brand new cocaine colored Cadillac Escalade, parked on a side street near one of his blocks as Bruno castigated him.

"Hey asshole, look at me when I'm talking to you!" Bruno snapped, "where's the fucking broad you brought with you to my stúnod brother's pool party last week?"

Roy didn't know what Bruno was talking about and looked perplexed the more Bruno became infuriated.

"Sammy was fucking arrested yesterday cause someone at the party took something they had no business touching! I suspect that broad you were with stole the goddamn videotape, since my sister-in-law caught her sneaky ass in the hallway acting like she was looking for the bathroom that night. So for shit's and giggles and to be on the safe side, take care of her ass."

Bruno started speaking to his passenger in Italian, "what did I tell you about trusting mool's in the house Vinn?"

Vinny sighed, shaking his head in disgust. He was a captain on the force as well as Bruno's muscle and didn't really talk that much.

"They sure don't make niggers like they used to Vinn, but this one is going to do the right thing isn't that right Roy boy? It's not too late for us if people start to disappear, know what I mean?"

Roy wasn't paying attention to what Bruno was saying as much as he wanted him to. The entire time the commissioner talked, Roy had been looking out of the rear window watching his workers make transactions.

"The right thing?" Roy questioned like an idiot, "What right thing Mr. G.?"

"Vinn smack him for me will ya'."

Vinny turned around and smacked the shit out of Roy like his superior told him to do.

"When commissioner Garliano is talking to you I want you to listen you fucking eggplant piece of shit! What he said was, you're going to whack that Indian Barbie doll with the pink Mercedes. Do you understand?"

Roy responded in a high pitched shook up voice, "What Indian Barbie doll? Kali? She ain't Indian, she's black"

"Come closer, a little further..." he lured, making Roy lean his head into the front seat.

Bruno then took his hand and applied full pressure to Roy's mouth squeezing it wide-open.

"I don't care what kind of nigger she is asshole!" Bruno yelled, with spit flying out the mouth as he pushed his fingers and thumbs harder into Roy's cheeks. "That's the problem with you jig's! You don't even realize that all you black people are fucking one family! Just take care of her or I'm going to take care of you!" Bruno threatened before releasing his grip.

"One of my guys tracked her license plate to

an address in Yonkers. But if she contacts you, do the right thing and make sure she's dead, got it? And since you have a listening problem, whack the teen on the tape too."

Vinny handed Dirty Roy a piece of paper with the 13-year-old's home address, but Roy pleaded for someone else to do the job.

"Come on man" his voice became desperate, "you're the fuckin' police, why can't you get one of your crooked ass rookies to do it. If I get caught killing a little white girl they'll put me under the jail" Roy protested.

Bruno shoved his cigar into Dirty Roy's neck causing him to scream like a sissy. Bruno became tomato red in the face from hollering at the top of his lungs.

"We let you earn a couple of bucks and now you think you own the goddamn city. You ungrateful bastard you, if you ever talk back to me again I'll leave you where I find you...Ka'pece! Now get the fuck out of my car, jack off, before I die out a pack of cigarettes in your fat cabbage head."

Roy hobbled out the Caddy, quickly pouring beer all over his neck to ease the burning pain. As the middle-aged Italians drove off, Vinny humorlessly exhibited the Black Power fist out the window mocking Roy's red black & green headband.

Even though Kali had Roy wrapped around her finger without giving him any pussy yet, Roy was terrified of Vinny and would do whatever they told him to do. Roy was 0 for 2 in getting things right. His first strike was vouching that Warren would make good on his debt to Garliano after they considered bumping him off. His second strike was bringing Kali to the private party with him.

# Scene Twenty-One

**The traffic in Harlem was ugly**. Cream decided to phone Drench to see what was up, while Shell drove 9 MPH up Broadway looking for Twana.

"What's the deal Tara? Drench home?" Cream asked D's sister when she answered the phone.

"NO he's not! And if you see his ass tell him I'm looking for him," she hollered with a stank attitude.

"Damn what's wrong with you? Just have him call me" Cream retorted, "if that's not a problem too!"

"I'm sorry Cream. I'm a lil' upset. I didn't mean to take it out on you baby. I'll tell D that you called if he ever shows up...okay sweetie?"

After Tara realized that she snapped at the man she had been trying to get with for years, she changed her tune quick, but Cream wasn't interested in her anyway.

"Thank you then, good-bye!" Cream hung up before Tara could say the same.

Drench wasn't home cause he was slumped over the steering wheel of an abandoned car that hadn't any doors or wheels. It sat on cinder blocks as just a pathetic frame of a car. Lying on the ground next to him was a bloodied aluminum bat that was used to beat him down last night.

Drench was dusted out of his mind again and attempted to walk home from a club he attended. On the way home he got into some shit trying to steal a carton of milk from a corner store. While attempting to run with the milk in his hand without paying, he ended up running around in circles demented from the crazy drug. The man behind the register grabbed his bat and fucked Drench up like he stole the store.

With 104 homicides in Bridgeport this year, Drench was lucky that he was not a statistic. He wasn't dead, but sure felt like it. The blows from the aluminum bat knocked him unconscious and swelled him up pretty bad. Two of the brutal Arab employee's dragged him around the corner onto Hamilton Street, so that their bootlegging business wouldn't be affected with a body lying on the sidewalk. After dumping him in the abandoned car they bounced.

Throughout the night Drench sat perched in the car out cold. Waking from his state of unconsciousness this morning, he was greeted with an ice-cold glass of milk. Drench grabbed the glass that Riva handed him and downed it. The milk dripped all over his shirt running off of his chin. For some reason milk brought a dust high down, but unfortunately he spent all of his money on drinks last night and wasn't able to purchase a carton. When he tried stealing one instead he got beat the fuck down in the process.

"What happened yo? You left me all hanging and shit. We waited for you last night but you never showed up," Riva stated aggressively.

Drench's memory was vague and right now he couldn't recall anything from last night, let alone Riva's sexy face.

"Riva...the girl from the club last night" she said, refreshing his memory.

"We were supposed to hook up after the club remember? I found you outside of my cousin house this mornin' lookin' a mess. I guess you walked over here! It looks like you had a fight and slept in that abandoned car all night," Riva laughed.

Drench looked completely lost. He never took into consideration that most of the time when he met women, he was usually drunk or spaced out on drugs. Riva was telling the truth about hooking up, but wasn't telling the truth about everything from last night. While her and a friend left to get their ride, Drench wandered out the club and tried walking to the address they gave him but got lost.

"One minute you're standing next to me, the next minute you're gone. I thought maybe you were just scared of this pussy," Riva sneered.

At one point in her young life, Riva was a highly attractive sister. But between all the pill popping and late night binge drinking she became a burn out. Time went by as Drench regained a sense of identity and what was going on. He laid on the couch holding his head as it pounded with pressure. Riva went on to remind him of all the outrageous things that he did in the club last night, while picking grass out of his hair.

"Was I really buggin' like that? I don't remember a damn thing," he confessed, as if acting crazy was something new for him.

Drench shook his head in utter disgust of himself the more Riva illustrated the evening for him.

"You were pushing through the crowd like a bouncer breakin' up a fight. Niggas got vexed and

I think they wanted to throw heat your way, but you kept on pushin' anyway. I bet you if Cream was there y'all would'a set shit off huh?"

*"Cream? How in the hell does she know Cream? I know I wasn't with him last night,"* Drench assured himself.

He continued to stare up at the ceiling holding the back of his neck. The reality of his ass whooping was certainly kicking in. Subsequent to sharing weed and accepting a few drinks from those in the club, Drench was prone to believe he could trust those people because they got high together. He had no idea that Riva slipped a mescaline in his drink last night, which caused him to bug out more than usual.

When Drench started running his mouth about the people that he knew and hung out with, Riva stuck to him like glue. After she found out he rolled with Cream, the person she was looking for, it was on. Jackie heard Laquan grumble about Ma'ati's new man Cream and planned on using Drench to get closer to him, which would lead her and Riva to their former comrade Ma'ati. Riva also had family in Bridgeport, but only planned on staying there until she caught up with Ma to settle their qualms and besides that the NYPD was looking to question Riva and Jackie for Laquan's murder.

"After you disappeared we almost killed that chick that kept sweatin' you all night. That bitch had the nerve to get all up in my face like you were her exclusive dick or whateva'! But the party was really over when my girl Jackie threw acid in that trick's face. Bitches started pulling out box cutters and throwing bottles and shit. It got crazy up in there and I was lovin' it!"

Riva may have appeared innocent looking, but she was really something treacherous. Drench tried his damnedest to remember the event but nothing rang a bell.

"Excuse me...its Riva right? Yo what did that chick look like?"

"I don't know," she jeered, "like a regular club hoe...tight jeans and a loose weave. One of those heifer's even had this stupid ass purple weave in her hair, lookin' like Barney and shit."

"Dark skin with big gold earrings?" Drench inquired, as his eyes got larger.

"Yeah that's her. I got them shit's right here!" Riva posed with one of the personalized earrings up to her ear.

"Who ever Tara is, she's gonna' be mad when I trade these shit's in."

Drench exhaled a long breath then reached for the pack of Newport's sitting on the coffee table, but Riva stopped him.

"Nah yo, I got one left" she objected, "and that's my special cig at that. My girl should be back soon. I know she bought a fresh pack just chill."

Riva neatly placed her cocaine-laced cigarette back into the box upside down. Two minutes later the doorbell rang repeatedly, "Ding! Ding! Ding! Ding!"

In came Jackie, another cokehead cutie pie who could sniff Grant's face off a fifty-dollar bill. She came in with a small bottle of Erk and Jerk in her hand, bent already and it wasn't even noon yet. Jackie's breath reeked of E & J and her eyes were bloodshot matching the rims of her nostrils.

"This ain't my crib so don't start bustin' up the place bitch! Have a seat next to my nigga Drench" Riva shouted, after Jackie almost knocked over her cousin's lamp.

"Your nigga?" Jackie objected, "I'm the one who fought over YOUR nigga last night. That's my dick sittin' on the couch."

Drench felt strange and looked like his mind was somewhere else.

"I just told you I'm good...get that shit out my face," Drench said after Jackie insisted that he take a sip of her E&J.

The screaming conversation Riva and Jackie got into gave him more of a headache than the one he already had. He was seconds away from smacking somebody until Jackie laid her head in his lap looking up at him with a drunken glare.

"Lets stop playing games yo. You said you know the nigga we lookin' for, so I'll give you some of this cho'cha if you give me what I need."

Riva rolled her eyes at Jackie for blowing up the spot.

"Excuse us Drench," she pulled Jackie in the kitchen by her bicep like an angry pimp would do if one of his hoes got out of line.

"You actually want to fuck this peezy head nigga don't you?" Riva argued with her teeth clamped, "business and pleasure don't mix, so keep in mind whose pussy that is between your legs! We really need this money and right now he's the only way were gonna' find Ma'ati to get it, so keep your mouth shut and let me handle it."

Jackie looked bemused as her girlfriend punished her with a tongue kiss and a slap on the ass. Drench overheard their whole conversation and sat back on the couch like he never moved when he heard them coming back. He was so out of it last night that up until now, he didn't remember that they agreed to give him some pussy if he helped them get with Cream.

"A deal's a deal," Drench stated with a new bold attitude, "so throw in some head and I can hook you up with my boy like we discussed."

"Who said anything about head?" Riva frowned then smiled, "I don't know about that, but you can tear my lil' ass out the frame for now."

Jackie had already taken a seat next to Drench on the couch. He started breathing heavy as she unzipped his jeans. After all that shit Riva was talking, she was the first one with her mouth on his dome.

"What'chu doin' Riva" Jackie garbled, "counting the veins in his dick? Let me see you swallow that whole thing like you made me do to Laquan," Jackie delightfully challenged, as she watched Riva's eye's roll back and her head move up and down like a chicken.

Drench was enjoying himself but was still bothered with the thought of his sister Tara getting acid thrown in her face by some crazy ass chicks plotting to set up his boy. He lifted Riva's head slowly off of him as she salivated all over his nuts.

"How about we get lifted at my crib" he suggested, "we can bang out there and get blasted at the same time. I got a half-gallon of Henny and an ounce of Dro too. I might even have some Yay, plus Cream usually stops by and I can introduce you to him then."

It was all bullshit. He actually had about a corner of Hennessy left and a few roaches that he kept around for rainy days. Jackie mulled over all of the different things they could do sexually, cause she loved wild threesomes and even more so when getting high was added to the mix. While the two females argued over which one would drive,

Drench underhandedly snatched his sister's earrings off the coffee table before they left.

Jackie's drunken ass ended up driving the charcoal gray Lincoln Navigator with the personalized license plate "Laquan." She drove like the Navi wasn't stolen at all, weaving in and out of traffic. They had lifted the truck after Laquan and his crew ran trains on both of them in his apartment. Following a parade of male orgasms, Riva lined up Laquan and all his friends against the wall and shot each one of them in the head. After they killed them, Riva and Jackie showered together then bounced to BPT with the little bit of money Laquan had in his apartment.

"Slow this shit down yo, you're blowing my high," Riva deliriously complained as the cocaine blast rushed through her lungs.

Jackie kept running lights anyway driving at a high rate of speed. Drench guided her to his spot without losing his temper.

"I can't wait to finish what you started," he said with a smile as he went inside first.

Two minutes later Drench waved them inside. Even though the State had just redeveloped half of the Garden, into condo-like project apartments after demolishing a few buildings, Drench's spot was already looking beat up. As the girls walked through the raggedy threshold, the smell of grease lingered in the living room.

"Pew!" Jackie grumbled, "was somebody gettin' a perm up in this piece? That shit stinks!"

"Don't worry about that baby, just get ready to show me that trick you were talking about in the truck...I never seen a pussy smoke a blunt before."

Riva inadvertently left her gun under the seat numb minded from the woolie she had just finished smoking. When they hit the bedroom Jackie started asking questions about all that liquor Drench said he had after she downed what was left of her E&J. To her benefit an opened half-pint was on the dresser.

"This is for my homies" Jackie giggled, spilling the cognac on Drench's hard-on as she repetitively poured and sucked.

It burned a little, but Drench let her have her fun. Riva collected the roaches that he had sitting in the ashtray, unraveling them on the bed to create one blunt. Both chicks were freaks, but Riva was truly bizarre. After she finished rolling the weed she used her clammy pussy to seal up the blunt.

While Jackie lay on the bed continuing to pleasure Drench, Riva blew smoke into her hole eating Jackie out as she used the empty Garcia Vega tube as a dildo.

"All this freaky shit got me hungry as hell," Drench stated after he quickly ejaculated.

"Keep doing y'all thing I'll be right back," he said, before turning up the stereo and closing the door behind him.

In the kitchen sat three anxious looking females with Vaseline all over their faces ready for revenge. There were two more in the living room with hammers in their hand. The one with her leg over the side of the couch gawked at Drench's physique as he stood ass naked and half-hard.

"Would you put on a towel please," Tara sneered at her brother, "before you give this girl a heart attack!"

"They're all yours," Drench asserted, "I got your earrings too, so don't worry about it."

Drench walked away to cover himself after

Tara gave him the message that Cream called and wanted him to holla' back.

What had actually happened in the club was nothing like Riva elucidated. Since Jackie and Riva were the last two people Tara had seen with her brother, she went over to them concerned about his whereabouts. Riva acted funny and expressed major attitude. Later on that evening, Tara accidentally bumped Jackie at the bar while ordering drinks when Jackie twisted her face as if to convey, "*not your ugly ass again*" and that's when she threw a acid drink in Tara's face. It had the kind of acid in it that one gets high from, like *LSD*, not the kind that burns your face like BPT chicks are known for throwing in the club. During all the confusion Riva snatched Tara's earrings off the bar and hit her in the head with an empty Grey Goose bottle.

Tara was still pissed about the whole thing, but cooled off a little. She wanted to teach Riva and Jackie that if you play with fire you might get burned. While the thuggish lesbians were in a 69 position oblivious to whose crib they were up in, revenge was on its way. Sheila, Tara's cousin, grabbed a butcher knife out of the drawer as the rest of the crew pulled out box cutters and held their hammers. It was on. Tara grabbed the hot comb that was on the stove and crept into her brother's room with the other girls behind her without alerting either one of the drunken broads.

Riva was on top with her ass arched upward facing the door, while Jackie's eyes were closed licking away. Tara casually placed the hot straightening comb up to Riva's fully spread out anal area.

"AAAAAAAAAHHHHHHHHHH!" Riva cried,

shrieking like a newborn baby.

Tara burned the shit out of Riva so much that urine shot out of her and the smell of burnt pubic hair filled the room.

"Surprise bitch! You didn't know Drench was my brother, did you stupid! Next time somebody asks you a simple question you should answer them!"

Shelia slapped Riva in the head with a hammer as she squirmed to the floor in excruciating pain.

"Your dyke ass better not move!" the girls yelled, while holding a butcher knife to Jackie's throat.

Jackie shivered with fear and her eyes swelled with tears in a failed attempt to get her blade out of her handbag. To add to her trepidation, one of the Garden girls used Jackie's own weapon to honor her with a buck 50 (razor slash) down the side of her face.

"That was for the scratches on my home girl's neck you dumb cunt!"

Jackie fell to the floor holding her face with both hands as the blood started to leak through the spaces between her fingers. Tammie, the one who was gawking at Drench in the kitchen, rushed into the room with a pair of barber clippers after she had taken the keys to Laquan's Navi. She parked it at the end of the street leaving the engine running and the doors wide open.

"Lets shave they're ass" the others voiced, at the same time punching and kicking Riva in her mouth.

Satisfied that they were baldheaded with permanent scars, Tara threw the petrified duo out of her apartment butt naked. They darted down the street, tits bouncing and all. The people outside just watched in shock, as two nude girls screamed uncontrollably in fear heading toward a truck with broken windows and flat tires. Making a spectacle of themselves caused the police to roll up and investigate their nudity in addition to the vandalized vehicle they attempted to drive away in. After the police ran the stolen Navigator plates, it was a wrap. Riva and Jackie were arrested and in all probability were going to be extradited back to New York for Laquan and his crew's murder.

# Scene Twenty-Two

**"BOOF!" The rim shook** and sounded, after being power slammed.

"In-his-face! Did you see the way he just dunked it on that scrub?" People screamed rhetorically as they watched legendary street ball players catch wreck at Rucker Park.

Bodies gathered all around the court, inside and out, cheering on the street stars. Warren gripped the fence with his face pressed against it watching the game from afar. Cream flinched when his cell phone vibrated, forgetting that it was clipped to his waist. It was Drench finally returning his call.

"Man I've been trying to reach you for a couple of weeks D, what's the deal?" Cream answered. "I don't know if you heard about Geek and Bing, but I just wanted to tell you to watch your back cause those niggas tried to kill me son."

"Word?"

"We don't know if it's over that Fat Jack shit or not, so keep your burner close and play it cool," Cream warned.

"That's funny you say that" Drench scoffed, "cause I was gonna' give you the same advice. I met these chicks last night that were looking for you and I think they had beef with you and your girl. Don't make me explain, Tara took care of it though" Drench exhaled sounding upset, "yo I knew you since sixth grade Yo, I thought we was click?"

"We is," Cream affirmed like what the fuck is talking about?

"Then when you gonna' put me down with some of that paper y'all gettin'? Big Danny and pink lip Dwayne are out here making mad money for War. Yo they got the block on flock! I heard after Fat Jack got bagged, War took over his shit. I knew y'all was getting' doe cause last month in the Motorcycle Club he lost five gee's in one hand like it wasn't shit!"

Cream was speechless as he stood next to Warren, while he talked on the phone. This was all news to him, even though he suspected that War was moving bundles out of Ma'ati's building. It was true that Warren was making big money, but most of it went into the pockets of the crooked Garliano police squad.

"Don't sweat it kid, I'ma hit you off, but you said someone was looking for me?" Cream inquired.

"Yeah these Brooklyn chicks I met. I was a little blasted and can't remember the whole thing, but I think they were really looking for some girl you're involved with. It must have been important, cause they gave me some pussy off the strength of my promise to arrange a meeting with you."

"I'm pleased to assist in your sexual affairs and I'm sure you enjoyed it, but let me call you back ai'ight? Keep a eye out D." Cream hung up and held on to the fence like Warren was.

"Yo we gotta' talk," Cream intervened.

"Count it...and the one, ooh!" Warren yelled

out, with full attention on the game.

"Yo you listening to me nigga?" Cream retorted.

Before he could question his mendacious partner's affairs, he noticed that Shell was getting into a heated argument with some candy girl on the sidewalk.

"Since I'm such a fuckin' lady" the woman yapped, "I'm not going to throw a brick through your windshield...Ceaser bought that shit for ME bee'otch! Not your Dolly Farton lookin' ass."

"I'll be a bitch" Shell taunted, "but it's in my name now honey, so you can kiss my ass and write a love song about it!"

Shell just laughed in the girl's face, but was dying to hit her with the heavy key chain that she held tightly.

The irate 24-year-old woman had a child in her arms and Shell knew better. Ma'ali broke it up before they could get physical with each other, as Cream and Warren came over to see what was up.

"Don't let me catch you by yourself Michelle," Ms Resentful threatened, walking away with her son in her arms.

"What was all that about?" Warren asked.

"Jealousy," Michelle answered, "straight up jealousy."

They got in the car and bounced after seeing that Twana was nowhere in sight. Warren was still curious as to what the squabble was about and kept probing.

"It was nothing baby really. She's just jealous of me cause I beat her to the punch."

Warren came with the 21 questions right away.

"You're worse than a cop," Shell said, "yes...

there was a man involved officer Hawkins."

"You sure it's 'was' and not still IS? I don't need some psychopath takin' shots at me cause he think he loves you and shit," said War.

"It's WAS Warren, I'm sure of that. His name WAS Ceaser. I really liked him a lot until I found out he was married with like ten kids and shit...all by different women at that. I should have known the deal because he was big in the streets."

"Get out of here?" War acted surprised, like Twana didn't already tell him a little something about Michelle's past.

"Anyway, he was married and told me that he was leaving his wife because she was cheating on him...go figure. My dumb ass believed him and we started seeing each other off and on for months. Then the day after I graduated nursing school, Ceaser sent a car to pick me up from my spot in Brooklyn. The driver told me it was important that I go with him. So I get in this Town car and there's a shiny stethoscope on the seat sitting on top of a note. There were flowers, chocolates, Champagne and a silver dome with peanut butter & jelly sandwiches underneath with the crusts cut off...he remembered the way I like them" Shell smiled, reliving the moment before continuing.

"Then we pulled up to this loft. I didn't have a clue what was going on. The driver handed me a set of keys telling me to follow the trail of gauze. One led to the truck we're in now and the other led to the loft entrance. There was a real-estate agent standing by the elevator and she told me all that she needed to complete the transfer was my signature. Fuck being gassed, I was full throttle and felt like super bitch!"

"Well, what happened next?" Cream asked, anxious to hear the rest.

"The note on the seat left instructions where to meet for dinner, but we can skip what happened after that. The next morning we...I'll skip that part too. Anyway I knew it was too good to be true. It always is. Five months later I found out about the army of kids and how Ceaser had done this with five other women before me. I mean I knew he hustled, but I didn't know his slick ass was makin' moves like that. He had keys to my apartment and was using the place as a stash house without me even knowing it. With spots all over the city, Ceaser thought he'd never get convicted. All of the apartments were in his girlfriend's names, so if the police ever raided all he had to do was deny everything to beat the charges. Unfortunately a lot of sistas ended up taking the weight for that devious son of a bastard...they were scared to testify against him cause he threatened to have their entire family murked."

Warren had a contemptuous look on his face after Shell started to wrap up her story.

"Not for nothin' Michelle, you still ain't tell me why that girl wanted to rip out your hair," Warren laughed.

"Oh that was one of Ceaser's jump offs. Come to find out, the bitch lived in my spot before I did. When she got pregnant," Shell snapped her fingers, "Ceaser cut her ass off like that! He was never planning to leave his wife at all. One day I went into his wife's hair salon to get my nails done. You know I wanted to see my competition...she was cute, not all that, but cute. What shocked me was how candid this bitch was. She was basically braggin' to her employees about how her husband uses dumb college girls to store his drugs and take the fall. I can't believe I was so silly to think he would actually leave his stinkin' ass wife for me? Her pompous ass didn't think it was so funny when her own sister filed a paternity suit and turned States evidence against Ceaser. Now her snooty behind is being investigated too" Shell laughed.

# Scene Twenty-Three

***H*alfway through a delicious meal** at the Shark Bar Restaurant in Manhattan, Ma'ati, Shell, War and Cream sat at the table sharing opinions about money and Rap stars after noticing a few patronizing the place.

"Don't hate cause they got more money than you nigga...if a man wants to cop twenty cars or spend a million dollars decorating his bedroom, let that man do his thing" Warren disputed.

"How am I hating? All I said was that sounds real ignorant to me!" Cream retorted.

"I agree with Cream," Shell said, "but I think they just don't know what to do with all that money. So I guess they shop all day...somewhat like myself," She tittered.

Needless to say Ma'ati was the one who stepped up the conversation on some analytical type of criticism.

"Come on Shell, you actually think MTV Cribs really cares how much money rappers spend on their ten car garage houses with gold plated driveways? Were gettin' clowned and don't even know it. They just want to show the rest of the world how silly black people carelessly spend their money. After watching programs like that, broke people scramble around, doing whatever they gotta' do just to keep up with the illusion of wealth. So you asked me what do I think about spending a million dollars on a platinum chain? Its your prerogative true, but it only reassures white America that they have nothing to worry about economically or otherwise cause the niggas gon' waste their money on bullshit."

"Excuse me" one of the waiters interrupted, "I hate to intrude, but the young lady sitting over there would like to take care of your bill, if that's all right with you all?"

Everyone turned around to see whom it was that wanted to foot the $140 check.

"Yo that's that chick with the pink drop top," Warren broadcast in disbelief.

Shell told the waiter that they'd only accept if she agreed to join them. Kali displayed a warm smile, while she waved her hand like Miss America. Cream couldn't believe that the girls knew each other either, and seemed bothered when Kali and her dinner date came over to merge. He thought the coincidence of meeting two women with pink Mercedes in the same summer, eating at the same restaurant was highly unusual. And at this point he felt leery of everyone at the table, Ma'ati included.

Kali greeted both of her friends with a tight hug and kiss.

"Look at you Michelle you go, those boots are fire girl!" Kali smiled, complementing Shell's outfit.

Kali was being modest, because her gear was like whoa. The canary yellow diamond-encrusted tennis bracelet that Kali rocked looked heavy on the wrist with the initials WH on it. The bling had caught Cream's eye especially, because he remembered seeing Ma'ati take the same exact bracelet out of her travel bag.

Kali drew the attention of all the men in the restaurant dressed in her black pleated satin skirt and knee-high stockings with a corset top that looked like it was painted on her body.

"I'm sorry to hear about Laquan," Kali expressed to Ma'ati, "we have to talk" she said, as she sat down sharing a blank look for a moment.

Kali jumped back into character after Dirty Roy gave the impression that it was odd for Warren and Cream to be sitting at the table.

"What'chu niggas doin' in the city?" Roy asked apprehensively as his eyebrow puckered.

Warren gestured back with a head nod and looked just as edgy as Roy, wondering who in the hell these girls really were.

"Are you going to introduce us to your friend?" Ma'ati cut in.

"My bad y'all, this is my pumpkin Roy...Roy Carter...the one I've been talkin' so much about," Kali introduced with a false smile.

"You mean pumpkin head," Shell muttered under her breath, noticing that Dirty Roy had an extra large forehead.

"Roy this is Ma'ati, Michelle and..."

"He knows who I am," Cream assertively spoke up for himself.

Roy kept asking questions regarding their reasons for being in the city. Before War could divulge too much information, Cream interceded.

"What, are you writing a fuckin' book? We're visiting family that's all, you got a problem with that!"

He didn't like anyone knowing his business and above all people Roy Carter. The word was out back home that Roy was a double-dealing informant, so Cream took heed and never forgot.

The girls just looked at each other suspecting a little tension between the two.

"What a coincidence you all know each other," Shell commented with a silly smirk. "Well since you're cool with each other, order some beers, while we head to the ladies room."

As soon as the three beauties entered the restroom, Kali made clear what was going on and why she asked them to meet her at the restaurant. She checked the stalls to make sure no one was listening before she continued to speak.

"It was Jackie and Riva that killed Laquan and his boys! I couldn't believe it when I seen that shit on the news...would you believe they were driving around in his Navigator like it was theirs and shit?" Kali exclaimed. "They were in on Mende's little plan to skip town with all our savings, but she double-crossed them too I see. I should've popped that psycho bitch when I had the chance."

Kali took a deep breath then vented some more. She was infuriated that her former colleagues attempted to run off with all of the group's resources.

"What did Laquan have to do with anything" Shell questioned, "Ma'ati told me Jackie was fuckin' him, but why'd she kill em'?"

"I'm guessing since Mende jerked them for their share of doe she stole from us, they decided to rob his ass to compensate the loss?"

"You're probably right" Ma'ati revealed, "Laquan had just received a large advance to record his album."

"I think we should take care of them two out there first, then track down Jackie and Riva. Lets save Mende's ass for last! What'chu think?" Kali asked. She had no idea that Riva and Jackie were now in police custody.

"What do you mean 'take care of them two out there'?" Shell inquired defensively.

"Michelle I don't know how you got involved with that Warren nigga, but he ain't right" Kali scoffed, "He tried to kill his best friend, so what makes you think he won't try to kill you when he finds out you know his M.O? Ma'ati will you tell your sista' what's up."

"Don't get mad at me Shell I just found out for sure after Kali called this afternoon. I knew Warren sold drugs out of my building, but I didn't know the police own his ass. Warren is indebted to them for stacks of cash. He was the one who set Cream up to get killed, so he could take his money just to pay them bastards!" Ma'ati explained.

"I don't want to stay in here too long arguing about who is what, so when we go back out there just follow my lead," Kali instructed.

...Fifteen minutes of pure girly gossip went by seated at the table. After she clicked off her cell, Kali tapped on one of the empty beer bottles with a fork, creating a bell sound.

"*Ting Ting Ting*...can I have everybody's attention. I just got off the phone with my record label and have to make an unscheduled trip. I didn't discuss it with my girls yet, but how does Miami Beach sound to you guys? They're shootin' a video down there and want me to be in it...with any luck you might be able to be in it too!"

"Miami sounds good, but are you asking us to go with you or are you asking us to sponsor the trip?" Cream grinned.

"That's the best part, the label's paying for everything," Kali replied with a straight face.

"You ain't gotta' ask me twice, you know I'm

wit it," Warren stated. The farthest he had ever been south was to Philly during the GreekFest, which turned out to be the weak fest. He was down for anything involving women wearing skimpy outfits.

Even though 20 minutes ago Cream felt leery about a lot of things, he figured spending time with Ma'ati away from the city couldn't hurt. Kali had Roy under the impression that she was signed to a major record label and was on the verge of blowing up. This gave some clarity and explained the high profile Kali and her girls presented. He wasn't so happy with the thought of Dirty Roy traveling with them, but he was still excited all the same. The only one indecisive was Roy. He seemed real cynical of the proposition.

"Come on baby, we could be laid out on the beach having fun..." Kali seductively pouted, "Don't you wanna' see me in that new thong I bought last week?" She asked.

Roy had no intention of actually going, but agreed just to shut Kali up. His plans were to kill her before the Garliano's killed him. Only problem was that ol' Roy boy was greedy and wanted to fuck Kali before he did the job. He even made sure that he kept all of the receipts from Kali's little shopping spree that he paid for this afternoon, so he could return the clothes and get his money back after he whacked her.

Before they hit the Shark Bar for lunch, Kali had Roy check into the Marriott Hotel in downtown Brooklyn. It really threw him off his game cause she led him to believe he was finally going to get some, after two months of teasing.

Kali said that they had to catch the next flight available, which was scheduled for departure at 7:00 PM leaving from LaGuardia, if they were to make the video shoot on time. It was 3:20 now and this would give them enough time to pick up a few travel items or whatever else they needed to take with them.

"Meet us at the Brooklyn Marriott in about two hours. I got some runnin' around to do myself. We can follow each other to the airport" Kali winked at Ma'ati, "make sure you bring a nice bathing suit."

As they left the restaurant Roy ended up paying for everyone's food like the sucker he was. Warren lagged three steps behind everybody else as they walked back to the car. He pulled Roy to the side speaking on the low, like he was in a rush.

"Tell that no neck muthafucka' to give me a little more time. I hope he didn't rent my block out to somebody else? Tell him that I ran into some problems with the money ai'ight."

"I guess you haven't heard...Sammy Garliano got knocked yesterday and I don't know how much longer Bruno is gonna' be accepting payoffs," Roy whispered in discontent, "I know he's gonna' start arresting niggas just to make himself look good."

As Cream walked over to see what they were talking about, Warren played it off like he and Roy were discussing something else.

"Yeah man, I love Lorna Doones too. Get me a lil' glass of milk with a good kung-fu flick... shhiiit!"

"I never knew you and Roy were so close" Cream snickered after Roy hopped in with Kali.

They headed down to Greenwich Village supposedly to pick up a new bathing suit and some other items that Shell wanted to get. She had this particular bikini store in mind, but changed it after spotting something else as they drove past other shops. The sisters went in one store, while Cream and War hit another. They planned to meet back at the $10 an hour garage that Shell parked in.

"Look at this one" Shell uttered, "Warren will cum on himself if he sees me in this shit!"

The mannequin they stood in front of displayed a Gucci g-string on its ass, similar to dental floss.

"Why wear anything at all?" Ma'ati stated sarcastically, "I have a ball of string at home that you can use instead of spending your money."

"Were talkin' Miami girl...the chicks down there dress like Luke dancers. I wanna' blend in real nice...know what I mean?"

"Yeah I know what'chu saying, but you act like we're actually goin'. You can snap out your role now," Ma'ati reminded Shell.

She also let her sister know that if they were to go on an exotic vacation, the only person she would intend on letting see her butt cheeks wiggle would be Cream anyway. The bogus trip just gave Shell another excuse to shop. She bought a pair of Gucci sandals to match the outfit that she picked out, including a matching towel to wrap around her waist for some other time.

Cream and Warren shopped in one store and both figured that their shirts would be off most of the time, either soaking up the sun or rolling around the bedroom. So they just snatched up some button-down linen shirts, boxers and a few jeans and fatigues. After the pushy salesman convinced Cream to buy the new Timberland arrivals, they headed back to the garage.

Walking down Sixth Avenue, Cream stopped to look at the table of books. Being thoughtful of

Ma'ati's interest he took his time going through the titles.

"Yo you got something on the Illuminati?" Cream asked the brother vending.

"Which one should I get yo," Cream contemplated, "Bloodlines of the Illuminati or Pawns in the Game?"

"I don't know, get both of them shit's so we can bounce," Warren complained.

War had the attention span of a tennis ball and could really care less what Cream bought for his lady. Cream paid the bookseller, giving the nod that it was okay to keep the change.

"That reminds me...who stung you in that black jack game last month?" Cream probed, "you lost a lot of doe I heard and I should punch you in your face for lying to me."

"What are you talking about man I never lost five gee's at the Motorcycle Club" War disputed, "And the day you punch me in the face is the day you get your ass kicked nigga!"

Cream raised his right eyebrow after testing Warren's honesty.

"I never said how much you lost or where you lost it, so you just told on yourself" Cream mocked, "fuck it though, if you wanna' play the drug-dealer roll, play it!"

Cream was silent for the entire walk back to the garage. He knew War was on some new shit after seeing how friendly he and Roy got along even though Warren knew about Dirty Roy being a snitch. For the first time in his life Cream was starting to have ill feelings that his lifetime PNC (partner in crime) could not be trusted.

# Scene Twenty-Four

**Surprisingly Michelle and Ma'ati** made it back to the Benz before Cream and Warren did. It was now 4:40PM and all they had to do now was stop by Shell's for a minute to pack a few things then meet Kali at the hotel.

Thirty minutes went by as they sat parked behind the Marriott on Jay Street in downtown Brooklyn.

"Damn were gonna' be late. Where the hell are they?" War protested, seeming anxious to get to the airport on time.

Out of no where, unmarked Crown Victoria's hastily pulled to the curb, one after the other, after the other. Police wearing thin nylon jackets jumped out with the letters "NYPD" on the backs, holding walkie-talkies in their hands as they eagerly scrambled to get inside the hotel.

Kali slipped right through the commotion calmly strolling over to Shell's Benz across the street. From a distance it appeared as if she was talking on the phone with her cell between her ear and shoulder, but as she got closer to the truck they could see that Kali was holding a balled up shirt to her neck. Warren noticed that in the restaurant her hair was braided in wide cornrows, but now it was tousled with wild curls like she had been in a fight. Her provocative skirt was torn and there was blood all over her arm.

"Hurry up, will you let me get in!" Kali exclaimed, forcing herself into the tight SUV. She carried with her a big sports bag as she climbed into the back.

"What the fuck is going on? Where's Roy!" Warren asked intensely.

"Aw shit! Kali you're bleeding" Ma'ati shouted, "Where'd you park the car?"

Cream didn't know what was going on at all or what to do. He was in awe of the situation, especially since Kali never answered Warren's question about Roy.

"Here! Take the keys" Kali instructed, groaning in pain, "it's parked in the lot on the second level" she said, "go around to the front quick before they lock it down!"

When Ma'ati hopped out, Cream followed right behind her. They tried to play it cool, but nervous as can be with all the paramedics and police scurrying outside the hotel.

"Meet us at my place!" Shell said, before flooring the gas all the way to the Manhattan Bridge, which was less than two blocks from the Marriott.

"Slow down Shell! You're gonna' make us look hot. Drive normal before we get pulled over," Kali gasped for air.

It was obvious that they weren't going to make it to the airport. Warren was pissed at himself for leaving his gun at Shell's place. The slice on Kali's arm wasn't as deep as it looked, but the slash on the side of her neck down to her chest was pretty bad. It was bleeding profusely even with the black t-shirt she held pressed on it. Kali definitely needed stitches or she was going to bleed to death.

Back in the hotel room, Dirty Roy was face down on the bed choking on his own blood, compliments of Kali's straight razor. He never got the chance to play out his plan of raping Kali first then killing her. Being a police captain, Vinny had people that worked for Equifax and when Roy used his credit card to get the hotel room this afternoon he was notified. Vinny had just as much to lose as his superior did, so he decided to take care of things himself. He drove to Brooklyn and waited at the hotel for their return to kill both of them.

When Roy and Kali got back to the hotel, Roy rushed to the bathroom to take a shit. That's when Kali heard a knock at the door.

"*Hotel manager, open the door please.*" As she slowly opened the door, Vinny forced his way inside. With no delay he threw her to the floor. Reaching into her bra Kali pulled out her father's straight razor that she kept on her person since he died. She vigorously struggled with the brawny Italian, cutting herself in the process of escaping his clutches. Underestimating the petite beauty's upper-body strength, Vinny got flipped to the floor when he grabbed her from behind. As he stood up Kali spun around, cutting his throat in the same motion one would throw a Frisbee.

Roy burst out of the bathroom with his jeans down to his ankles in a nervous panic when he saw Vinny lying on the carpet. He dove for his gun on the nightstand. Kali leaped at the same time, slicing his throat before he was able to grab the weapon. Roy didn't even realize he was cut and let off one shot before collapsing. He fell face down into the bed holding his throat like he was choking himself, as he gargled blood. The occupants in the other room called the front desk after hearing the shots, and naturally officers were dispatched to the scene.

Shell got to her spot in about ten minutes by taking the Manhattan Bridge. Warren didn't want to, but he helped carry Kali inside anyway. After they laid her on the couch Shell retrieved her first aid kit to stitch up Kali's wounds. She was trained for this type of trauma being a RN and all. Kali had passed out in the truck and was coming in and out of it since then. Shell returned with nutmeg, towels and a big bottle of Betadine.

"I'm going downstairs to get the rest of our stuff..." War yelled from the other room.

"Good, you could bring up my purse. I need my small tweezers out of there," Shell enunciated.

She was paying attention to what she was doing and forgot what they discussed at the restaurant about Warren.

"You're gonna' be fine Kal I know it hurts girl just try and relax" She said, coaching Kali as she shifted with pain.

Kali was trying to warn Shell about Warren handling her bags, but passed out in the process. Ma'ati and Cream weren't so lucky with traffic. Instead of taking the Manhattan Bridge, which exits in Chinatown. Ma took a left turn onto the Brooklyn Bridge cause it looked less congested and mistakenly switched to the FDR Drive ramp. Like usual the traffic was stop and go.

"What do you think happened to Roy?" Cream yelled, reflecting on what just went down.

He had to yell cause they were both having a hard time hearing each other with the drop top down in the middle of traffic.

"By the way Kali looked, I'm sure he's dead" Ma'ati bluntly responded. "Your boy Dirty Roy was, um...dirty. He was a Black Sweep stoolie."

"You mean Warren's boy!" Cream corrected her.

Ma'ati elaborated briefly about what she knew about *Operation Black Sweep* as they exited the FDR. Before they got to Shell's, Ma'ati pulled over on Greene Street to talk for a minute. She locked eyes with Cream before she spoke.

"I know you don't wanna' hear this baby, but Warren is dirty too...He's not a snitch as far as I know, but he's a double cross liar. Not only is he selling drugs in my building, but the whole thing about his aunt gettin' beat up by Fat Jack was bullshit! He just wanted to make a move on Jack's drug business with your help. I thought you were down with it too, until I learned otherwise. Kali just told me today that she found out that Warren was the one behind those niggas trying to kill you. She heard him and Roy talkin' about it on the phone she said."

"How do you know all this, you act like you've been following him or something?" Cream asked with suspicion.

"We did and we followed you too! Look I have a lot to explain...I just hope you understand."

Ma'ati confessed to Cream in the short time it took to get to Shell's, everything that she hid from him. She admitted to being part of an all female clique, confidentially known as The Woman Hood.

*The Woman Hood was really inspired by Kali's father and was ignited after his death to vanquish the debauchery that had spread. Kali was born and raised in the Brownsville section of*

*Brooklyn, not too far from her father's best friend Akoben, Ma'ati and Shell's father. Their fathers were tight because they served in the Vietnam War together. Tawi would visit Akoben all the time bringing his little girl along to play with Ma'ati and Shell. However they never got along with Kali until they were in their teens.*

*When Tawi heard of the news that his buddy was going to prison trying to protect his family, he acquired a bitter attitude toward life. He really blamed the U.S government for treating Vietnam veterans the way that they did and also for employing the drug pushers that took over the hood. He would preach on the corner that selling drugs was temporary Federal employment, in which you don't even know that you work for the government. You get paid under the table and there are no benefits, he would criticize.*

*Tawi and Akoben were two of the very few soldiers that weren't addicted to drugs when they returned from the war. Ironically though, Kali's mother was strung out on coke when he came home. Between being ignored and building frustration, Tawi formed a group of black veterans that were all from the Tri-State area. They all served with each other and called themselves the VETS. The VETS started killing drug dealers, malicious addicts and crooked cops as if they were back in Vietnam. Big time dope dealers were found dead all over the city. Some turning up in dumpsters and others left floating in the East River.*

*Witnessing the destruction of black civilization over the years took its toll on each and every one of the VETS, causing this outburst of vigilante rampage. Especially since they fought overseas to uplift the lives of their families, only to come home to a world of shit. Being a sharp shooter in Nam, Tawi had an arsenal of high-powered rifles at his disposal. The other vets had a magazine of weapons too. They would meet every week either in Tawi's small project apartment or in Johnny Red's basement on Sutter Avenue discussing the regiment's progress. Kali would watch them as they cleaned their weapons and eventually learned how to use all the different types of assault rifles and handguns.*

*The newspapers ran headlines such as, "The Brooklyn Sniper strikes again" and "The Real War on Drugs," after they began shooting dealers from the roofs of project buildings. Years of faithfully visiting his best friend Akoben upstate suddenly stopped. Tawi didn't forget about his comrade in prison, he just decided to mail the newspaper clippings to speak for themselves instead of complaining about how perilous the streets had become. Action speaks louder than words.*

*Time went by and more and more thugs were left on the ground where new ones now stood. The VETS agreed that they were getting nowhere with the way they were going about things, because as soon as they took out one dealer, two more appeared to take his place. So they began buying drugs as a front to find out how high the ladder climbed.*

*At first the trail led to Harlem and it appeared as though the Dominicans had the drug game sewn up in NYC, but after taking down the multi-million Dominican drug organization, "HeYo YaYo," the Veterans got to climb even further. When they did, all they found out was that the same people that were supposed to be taking drugs off the streets, were the same ones incorporating the massive drug flow, funneling the hoods with poisons.*

*When the Vets got too close to top municipal and federal political figures, a standoff soon occurred in Brooklyn. An alphabet of government agencies initiated a raid, which led to the deaths of all six of the VETS and thirteen agents. The veterans went out in a blaze of gunfire just like their brethren in Vietnam.*

*Kali ended up living with her mother on Gates Avenue and by now her moms had graduated from coke to crack, compelling her to make it on her own. In the spirit of her father, Kali regenerated the VETS as the Woman Hood. She inducted Ma'ati as the first member beside herself. It wasn't hard convincing her friend to join, because she also lost her family over drugs and a criminal-Criminal court system. Ma'ati learned the art of guerrilla warfare that Kali taught her and also taught Kali a few things too.*

*At first they only dated local hustlers taking both their money and product. Sometimes they even took their lives. Then Kali stepped it up by pursuing big time willies that never seen her coming, being that they were blinded by her youthful smile and beauty. Between Kali and Ma'ati they must have taken out 22 big dawg drug dealers and 11 corrupt cops, accumulating almost $300,000 cash in two years. After awhile they failed to remember why they were doing what they were doing and Kali almost slipped into the lustful world of materialism. There were a lot of less extreme organizations in Brooklyn at the time that were trying to ease the systems pressure, but needed funds. So Ma'ati came up with the idea to* *donate portions of the cash they seized to underground grassroots organizations, like S.E.E.D.S, a program that helped children whose parent or parents were incarcerated.*

*A year went by before Kali recruited other women whom the streets had used and abused. Two years following the Woman Hoods conception, they were 13 deep. Each one learned quickly what Ma'ati and Kali taught them. In the blood-sucking underworld of drug dealing, the sexy hit squad dealt payback instead of dope. There was one major stipulation that Kali now imposed; Any money confiscated from a target, except the necessary amounts needed to maintain their alluring image, goes to the Clique's list of Grassroots organizations and 10 % into the groups savings fund.*

*That agreement didn't last very long after recruiting this wild stripper who danced at Sue Rendezvous, a strip club in MT Vernon. Mende was her name and she took splurging to another level. Prior to meeting Kali, Mende was doing her thing, but began living more lavish than the dealers they were exterminating. Seeing how Mende was living it up after joining the Woman Hood, the rest of the girls in the group became jealous and lustful for more cash to spend on themselves. Riva and Jackie tried to mimic Mende's savoir-faire, but were too coked out to pull things off like she did.*

*The spirit of cleaning up the streets completely went out the door after Mende came into the equation. Most of the girls in the Woman Hood dressed like Divas as it was already, wearing expensive jewelry and luxurious designer clothes on the regular and after Mende's influence they went far beyond the call to fashion.*

*Kali came up with the idea of allowing each of the members to purchase any type of vehicle they wanted, no matter the cost as long as they had it painted pink to somewhat satisfy their longing to splurge and shine. She was bugging like the Woman Hood was Mary Kay or something and the idea didn't work anyway. After all the good intentions, the Woman Hood had now become a trained group of cutthroat females out for themselves. Fatally, this behavior led to the deaths of five members who tried copying the new girl's style of dealing with niggas, which was the straight up "stick up kid" approach.*

*Mende fled the Tri-State solo, loaded with almost $200,000 in cash that she stole from the group's savings fund, which was stored in Kali's crib in Yonkers. Mende's double cross plot left Riva and Jackie in search of more unsuspecting drug dealers to brutally rob and murder to fulfill their Champaign dreams of being filthy rich.*

*Growing up as a teen Shell stayed in school and didn't hang around her sister and Kali that much and was never officially inducted, so besides her there were only three faithful members left. Kali, Ma'ati and Toya. Toya wasn't around only because she had got convicted with one of her targets and was now doing two to four in a federal prison. Toya and Kali were real tight and planned to hunt down Mende and the rest of the chicks that betrayed the Hood when she gets out.*

*There were also twins in the group who had disappeared too, but they had nothing to do with Mende's trickery. After everything fell apart, Kali and Ma'ati decided to relocate to Connecticut to start all over again and find clues as to where Mende could have went. They figured since*

*Bridgeport wasn't as large as any of the boroughs in NYC, they could handle it, but they underestimated the grimy streets of the Bang Bang also known as Bridgeport.*

Once Ma'ati finished explaining the history of the Woman Hood and the rest of the loose ends dangling in her life, Cream could only sit back and smile, imagining all the lawless things his sweetheart did in the name of reciprocity.

"The only reason we targeted you" she said, "was because you seemed to be a big name on the Ave when we first came out there. When I actually met you and seen how you got down, I knew you weren't such a terrible guy."

"How do you know," Cream responded, "I might be a killer? What'chu think I look soft?"

"I think you're a well balanced person with a good heart, so save the tough guy act for the card tables killa'!"

The Woman Hood was really the sum and substance of how drastic situations had become since the crack attack. The only way the black man and woman were to make it through the perils of injustice and an evil empire, was to fight side by side and stay together. In the unwavering battle for peace and tranquility females took to the battle field. Ma'ati was now Cream's Balance and he needed her more than ever.

"If we're going to be together I want you to think of us as two halves making up one whole. You don't have to do everything by yourself," he corroborated, after Ma confirmed that she needed help, "men and Women are not opposite each other, we're rather the compliments of each other

Cream said he thought it was a man's job to be on the frontline before a woman, because women are naturally nurturers and men are naturally protectors. He said switching roles like that disrupts the family arrangement.

Finally parking the car, Ma popped the trunk and they each grabbed a bag, promptly making their way upstairs. Cream didn't have any bitterness toward Ma'ati for not telling him the truth earlier. He was rather turned on because he had finally met his dream girl; a pretty face intellectual sista' with a bangin' body that could kick ass at the same time if need be.

# Scene Twenty-Five

**Kali was still on the couch,** not resting but tied up now. After Shell had cleaned and stitched her injuries like a professional doctor would have, Warren came back upstairs flipping the script. He started going off smacking Shell around like a dude. He wrapped panty hose around both girls wrists then laid Shell face down on the floor.

With suspicion that Kali was following him already, Warren confirmed his feeling after accidentally spilling Kali's bag on the ground, while bringing her bags and stuff upstairs. There were all kinds of guns and surveillance gadgets inside. One of them contained dossiers in manila folders containing exclusive information on a wide range of people.

Warren picked up one of the pictures that he had stepped on, after noticing it was a photograph of himself with Dirty Roy leaning on a car. There was even a Polaroid with him and Cream posing in front of a graffiti painting inside of a nightclub flashing money. Most of the other pictures were stapled to pieces of paper with notes attached.

War became nervous pacing back and forth, wondering who in the hell Kali really was.

"Sit still and shut the fuck up! I don't know

how you know all my business, but you're lucky I don't kill you right here" Warren yelled at Kali, as she made a great effort on the couch to get free.

He poked her in the back real hard with the nozzle of her own gun then he walked over to Shell with Kali's P-90 sub-machine gun in his grip lifting her up off the floor.

"Tell me who you're working for, or she's dead! Is Garliano behind this? What are all these pictures and guns for, ha?" Warren yelled as he pulled Shell around the apartment threatening to kill her.

Shell looked intently at Warren with a soul-shattering stare in her eye. If looks could kill he would have been cremated.

"Fuck it, I know you rich bitches got money up in here. Just tell me where it's at and I won't kill you. I was really starting to like you Michelle. Will you stop looking at me like that, I'm not gonna' kill you, just tell me where the money is baby," Warren begged like a fiend.

He demanded that they tell him where the speculated stash was hidden, but Shell couldn't say anything cause War had surgical tape tightly wrapped around her mouth. He ripped it off like a wax peel so Shell could talk. Immediately she screamed in a fit of anger.

"Baby! Baby my ass nigga! Fuck you Warren I hope those cop's you owe stick a bazooka up your muthafuckin' ass!"

"I'll pop you if I have to Shell don't push it."

Warren walked her upstairs to make sure she wasn't lying when she told him that there was no money in the house. He dumped out Shells purse onto the bed in disappointment, because between Shell and Kali there was only $1300 in cash and mad credit cards. When they got back downstairs Kali had rolled off the couch onto the floor, squirming her way into the kitchen.

"Where you think you goin'?" War said as he ripped Kali's shirt some more dragging her back into the living room.

The apartment looked a mess. Everything was ransacked with papers and clothes all over the place. After hearing the elevator's squeaky safety gate rise up, Warren positioned himself at the side of the freight elevator outlet, forcing Kali to lie next to Shell on the floor. As soon as Ma'ati stepped out of the elevator, he violently grabbed her by the arm pointing the big ass P-90 up to her head.

"Drop it like it's hot or say good night to Ms. apple bottom!" Warren commanded Cream.

Cream didn't listen and kept his gun pointed straight ahead. Warren shoved the sub-machine gun harder into Ma'ati's temple and Cream still didn't budge. He circled as War rotated around the room holding Ma'ati as a shield.

"I knew you for years" War shouted, "you're willing to die for some chick you just met? She was going to kill you like her girl killed Roy. Look at those papers on the floor...don't be stupid nigga, put the shit down I'm not playing," he threatened Cream one last time.

From the hardcore look Cream displayed, Warren could tell that his betrayed friend was not going to put his gun down anytime soon. Cream was willing to die protecting the woman he fell in love with. War grabbed the car keys out of Ma's hand then pulled her back toward the elevator.

"I know all about Tootsie and Fat Jack Warren you lied...I even know about Bing-O and Geek. I never conned you nigga, so what made you wanna' see me dead? Was it money?" Cream asked, "you're a back stabbin' mound of shit you know that!" Cream hollered, intently aiming Ma's .380 at Warren's head, while War now held his gun to Ma'ati's chin.

"Do you know how many times I stopped niggas from robbin' your ass on the Ave? Be happy I let you live this long" War nervously laughed.

Warren had informed Bing-O and white boy Geek that Cream was stacking money. He even told Geek that Cream was the one who robbed Fat Jack for a large amount of cocaine. Then he said if they killed him he would hit them off with some of the product and also give them $5000 a piece. Warren wasn't going to give Bing-O shit. After he finagled the money out of Cream's aunt's house, he planned on shooting him and Geek anyway.

Fat Jack had nothing to do with the attempt on Cream's life at all. Jack never beat up Warren's aunt like he said, but instead they were going through a nasty divorce. Warren made up the whole thing just to have Cream help him rob Jack, so he could blame him for everything if niggas brought the beef to his ass. War went down hill last year when he had got caught with a bundle of dope and a pistol that had a body on it.

Nobody knew about War's run in with the police except for him and Garliano's crooked underlings. To stay out of prison Warren agreed to pay the $15,000 the police crew charged for what they called the "exonerating bad behavior fee." Subsequent to paying them once, Warren was shook down for more and more. It was a never-ending debt and eventually Warren was turned into another Dirty Roy.

"I never wanted it to go down like this"

Warren declared, "but I told your ass before that cash rules everything around this muthafucka! You didn't listen. I had a choice to either pay them or do ten years...if you can't beat em' join their ass...now drop the goddamn gun Cream and hand over the doe in your pocket."

Cream tossed him the rubber banded wad of hundreds and was about to give up his gun.

"Don't give him your gun!" Kali yelled, "he'll kill everybody after you do!"

When Warren moved his gun away from Ma'ati's head to aim it at Kali. Ma'ati elbowed him in the gut before he fired, then threw herself to the floor. Cream charged forward firing nonstop at Warren. The P-90 blew a dinner plate size hole in the wall right above Kali's head. Cream had grazed Warren in the shoulder before he ran down the emergency staircase into the street. War swiftly hopped into the hot pink Benz, pulling off even faster. The car was hot in more ways than one because by now the police had an all points bulletin out on it.

"Ma'ati you okay..." asked Cream, as he lifted her off the floor.

"Yeah I'm straight, help Kali and Shell."

Cream untied their panty hose cuffs then helped Kali back onto the couch. She started bleeding again from one of her previous wounds that reopened when Warren forced her on the floor. Shell had tears of anger, not really saying anything at all.

"Don't even try to follow him," Kali scoffed, "if he took the AMG he won't get far. The New York pricks and dicks (NYPD) should be looking for a pink drop top by now...the funny thing is, that shit wasn't mine anyhow," Kali laughed into a cough, because the pussy pink Mercedes was originally Mende's, but she was left with it after Mende skipped town.

Warren made it all the way to the FDR in three minutes. Just as he hit the entrance ramp, two squad cars and a police van flashed their lights. He floored the sports car resulting in his cap blowing off since the top was down. At a high rate of speed he hit two cars in the third lane trying to escape. There was no way around the stop and go traffic by the Queens Borough Bridge exit and at 85MPH the AMG came to a screeching halt smashing into a cement barrier.

"Buck! Buck! Buck! Buck! Buck!" Shots echoed through the underpass as Warren ran north with a Jansport book bag.

He ran at top speed firing backwards at the cops that were chasing behind him 10 yards away. The police received hostile reports about the Marriott murders and were firing to kill. They shot Amadou Diallo over 41 times just for reaching for his wallet, so you know they were trying to blow Warren's head off.

Traffic was at a complete standstill. People stopped in the middle of the expressway to duck down in their vehicles trying to avoid flying bullets. War caught one in the arm and stopped running to hide behind a stopped Suburban. The large P-90 fell out of the book bag after he tripped in a pothole. His 9mm was out of ammo, so he tossed it and picked up the brolic submachine gun and let it spray.

"BLLA'DAAT! BLLA'DATT! BLLA'DATT!"

Bullets hit everything and everybody as he waved the assault weapon in a 180-degree blast radius. One of the cops that were chasing him on foot was spread eagle on the hood of a car smoking from the chest. The other one collapsed after the missile like rounds ripped through his vest like cotton. About five passengers in their cars got hit as well.

War wasn't free just yet. There were a dozen squad cars blocking all exits for escape. He took off running again, clutching the book bag in his hand dripping with sweat and out of ammo. Panicking and desperate to escape, he started pulling on car doors as the last means to get away. He chose the wrong car to jack when he opened the door to a 1994 Honda Accord. The young bloods inside let loose their blinkys, filling his body with hot lead. While Warren was getting shot, it looked like he was doing the Harlem Shake, as the bullets tore through his muscular frame. In the last breath of his life he tightly held on to the knot of cash that he took from Cream.

# Scene Twenty-Six

**Months went by since the grave drama** in New York took place. Cream ended up giving Warren's mother enough money for his former friend to be buried and at least have a head stone, since Warren didn't have any life insurance. War's moms was dead broke and none of his other alleged partners coughed up any doe, so Cream felt it was the right thing for him to do.

Given that Shell's lease was up, Kali had invited the sisters in company with Cream, to stay with her at her hide away Yonkers home until things blew over.

It was Sunday and Kali was in her room jotting down notes in between packing a few clothing items. Before joining everyone else in the living room, Kali rubbed some Shea butter on her razor scars, examining herself in the mirror. She playfully hugged and kissed Shell, thankful again that the slashes on her neck didn't Keloid.

Ma'ati was laid up with Cream on the couch talking about how much she would really enjoy taking a vacation somewhere exotic like the Travel Channel was presented on TV.

"I promise baby," Ma'ati nibbled on Cream's ear, "before the twenty-first of December we're going somewhere hot."

"You can get soft and mushy on your own time, in your own place," Kali said as she stepped in the room, "instead of playin' Mr. & Mrs. lovey-dovey all day, you should be thinking about how you're gonna' fix up the building I purchased for you miss...thang."

"Wait a minute Kali...you didn't," Ma'ati beamed a smile.

Kali was just as thrilled as Ma'ati was, subtly dropping the surprise on everyone.

"It's a real hell hole trust me, but the foundation is still good. You can finally build that revolutionary day care center you always talk about. And since you said you were nice with the hands Cream, you should be able to do most of the labor" Kali laughed.

"How could you afford to buy a building?" Cream asked, as if he knew Kali's financial status.

"It wasn't that easy let me tell you...I had to put up one whole dollar to close the deal," she ridiculed, "four quarters."

Kali explained that Bridgeport had lots of decrepit abandoned buildings all over the city that they were getting rid of for $1. If the purchaser agreed to live on the premises and pay any back taxes, the property was theirs. It was all part of some rehabilitation strategy going on nationwide.

The prospective property was just three blocks from Cream's aunt's house and only two streets over from where Ma'ati's Grandmother once lived. With apartments on top of storefront space, it was the perfect thing for them to build a relationship together and set in motion their quest to restore optimism in the hood. Kali made clear that the building was dilapidated and that there was still $9000 owed in back taxes. Cream figured the refurbishing would probably cost thousands too, but was still well worth it in the long run.

Ma hugged Kali real tight and thanked her for being such a go getting person in her life. In their mutual exchange of accolades, Kali acknowledged Ma'ati as being the balancing force in her chaotic world and admitted that she learned a lot about life from her as well. Shell joined in the delight, sharing various ideas about the property's potential.

"I have to make a run" Kali interrupted, "I have a few errand's to take care of. So why don't y'all look over the paperwork and discuss whatever you have to discuss, while I step out for a minute."

Shell offered to give her a ride but Kali refused. She thanked her one more time for suturing her wounds, while stuffing a big Samsonite travel bag into the back of her real ride, a triple black painted Cayenne Turbo SUV.

After Kali left, Ma'ati helped Shell fix a banging dinner for everyone instead of going out to eat. She said she had a big surprise to share, but wanted to wait for Kali to return. They really got down cooking all types of vegetables with baked fish and even did up some honey biscuits.

Hours went by and Kali hadn't returned. She said that she'd be back soon and three hours had passed already. They were getting worried. Shell walked into the kitchen with an envelope in her hand that she found taped to the bathroom mirror. The name Tiara was written on the front, so Ma'ati opened it and read it aloud.

*"If you're reading this note I guess you're wondering where I am right now. I'm fine. I had to pay Sammy Garliano a visit since all charges*

*against him were dropped. I can't wait to hear him beg for his life. More importantly congratulations Ma'ati! I'm letting you know right now that I want to be the godmother and I hope it's a boy! I found the EPT in the wastebasket if you want to know how I found out before you told me. The reason I left a note instead of saying goodbye in person, is because I'm not saying goodbye at all. You know I'm not good at saying goodbye anyway.*

*Girl you and Cream are in love. It's written all over both of your faces. I think you should give the Woman Hood a rest for a while and pick up on living the life you missed trying to save the world. You told me once that your father always said 'the life you save may be your own', so I'm passing that advice on to you. I think you need it more than me right now. Don't worry, Kali is gonna' do Kali.*

*I still can't believe you're pregnant! So now more than ever, we can not afford for you or Shell to get hurt. If I told you I was going to track Mende and them other back stabbing bitches down after I take care of Garliano, you would have either wanted to go with me or tell me to let it go. It's not about the money at all if that's what you're thinking, it's about payback! What goes around comes back around and this bitch is coming for their ass!*

*Anyway girl you and Shell are beautiful smart young women, but there's one thing I think you're missing out on and that's the grandeur of life being a Woman. (Don't get gassed thinking I read all those books you gave me, cause I just got that word out the dictionary.) Just let nature take its course and please let Cream protect you instead of trying to do everything by yourself. I'm not gone for good so take care of my spot for me. I left some money in my room and it should be more than enough to get you started and cover my bills. If you want to, you and Shell can stay there, while your luv bug Cream gets his ass busy renovating. By the time he's finished I should be back and you should be ready to deliver my godson. Give Shell my love and take extra care of the baby starting right now, do you hear me! Don't worry, change is good cause it's inevitable and who knows, I might even meet someone too...we can get twin mountain bikes and ride the countryside holding hands with our men...Yeah* right!

*ONE LUV*
*Your girl Kali"*

Ma'ati stared into thought after reading Kali's note then smiled at her sister releasing tears of both joy and sadness.

"Ma'ati this is wonderful!" Cream shouted, "I'm gonna' be a father! I can't believe it! I'm gonna' be a father," he continued to shout more and more, as he ran over to feel his queen's flat belly.

"I don't know how to say this baby...but I'm not pregnant. I would love to have children with you someday, but I'm not the one," Ma'ati sorrowfully voiced looking at Shell.

"I wanted to surprise all of you over dinner" Shell clarified with tears, "so guess what anyway...I'm having a baby!"

She sighed with her hands in the air trying to act happy, but it was obvious that she was still depressed about what happened with Warren. She burst into tears as Ma'ati hugged her.

*How am I going to tell my child that it's father tried to kill mommy before it was even born,* she thought. Shell never considered having an abortion and didn't believe in doing that anyway, so it shall be. Cream coupled the expectant mother along with Ma'ati, expressing the pain he also felt. Together,they made a solemn promise to Shell that they would be positive figures in her child's life. For Shell the bittersweet moment was brightened by the knowledge that the future was growing inside of her.

*Men are born to be heroes as our mothers and fathers already are. Let us as men, be true to the instincts within us. Let us be ourselves and restore our virtue. For until we do, we will never truly be men. Our mothers, grandmothers, and great grandmothers have sustained the battle, and as we rise from the flame completely a man, we thank you as you are the ones which are all Great and Grand .*

*Marcus Spears*

ALL is in all
and ALL is mind.
The Universe is mental,
boundless, without any
conception of time. So
deliver yourself out of
ignorance in each and
every way
and
if
you
may
be
so
kind
to
the rest of your family
each and everyday.

AMUN.

# ORDER FORM

Address to:
4Word Press P.O Box 6411 Bridgeport, Connecticut 06606

**www.4wordpress.com**

**PURCHASER INFORMATION**

Name:______________________________________

Inmate #:____________________________________
(necessary for institution orders)

Address:_____________________________________

____________________________________________

City: ___________State: __________Zip:___________

Total Number of Books Requested:_____Payback _____Behold

**Payback's A Bitch** $12.00 (SALE PRICE)

**Behold A Pale Whore** $12.00 (SALE PRICE)

**Shipping/Handling** $3.00
(Via U.S Priority Mail) ( ADD $1.00 FOR EACH ADDITIONAL BOOK)

**TOTAL**_____________________________ $15.00

For orders being shipped directly to prisons costs are as follows:

**Payback's A Bitch** **$11.00**
**Shipping/Handling** **$3.00** (add $1 for each additional book)

Accepted forms of payment include:
**Institutional Checks** or **Money Orders.**

**TOTAL**_____________________________ $14.00

PRICE & AVAILABILITY SUBJECT TO CHANGE WITHOUT NOTICE